the kingdom

JENNIFER M. BARRY

WWW.MARTINSISTERSPUBLISHING.COM

Published by

SkyVine Books, a division of Martin Sisters Publishing, LLC

www.martinsisterspublishing.com

Copyright © 2011 by Jennifer M. Barry

ISBN: 978-1-937273-49-1
Editor: Kathleen Papajohn
Cover Art: Natalie Pryor

Fantasy
Printed in the United States of America
Martin Sisters Publishing, LLC

DEDICATION

Special thanks to Melissa Fox, Tiff Nichols, Kristie Hoek, Tali Pryor, Niki Venis, Abby Wucherer, Eva Pugzlyte, Claire King, and Brandy Heineman for giving of their time, talent, and friendship; to my husband for his everlasting patience; and to my parents for unconditional love.

~ This book is always for Kevin, who waits at the gates ~

SKY VINE
BOOKS

an imprint of Martin Sisters Publishing, LLC

a caoineadh

I saw her before I ever heard her. That may be what will save me in the end, as I can recall my first glimpse of her. She didn't exactly stand out from all the people surrounding her, but I suppose there was something about her that drew me. Maybe it was her movements; they were graceful and unselfconscious. She had earphones in and was swaying gently to music that only she could hear. The riot of red curls would have easily stood out anywhere, but not in Ireland. In fact, besides her mindless movement, there was absolutely nothing remarkable about the girl with the flame-colored curls.

As I watch her take her last breath, that is what I remember— not her voice, for that would break me, and not her unfailing selflessness, for my mangled heart can only bear so much. No matter how battered I am, my heart will still beat. I remember her humanity, all the things that make her ordinary. I remember a girl, broken and yet perfect, who changed her world, and mine, with her love.

JENNIFER M. BARRY

a haon

Rare Irish sunshine bathed the quad at Trinity College in Dublin. Students who should have been worried about their final examinations were more concerned with getting that last bit of warmth before the clouds could roll in again. The lads wore T-shirts and shorts, and the girls wore as little as they could get away with. That was exactly why I loved the university.

I carried no books, save for my ever-present journal, but I still blended with the crowd. A brunette in a barely-there skirt caught my eye, and I winked to let her know I'd seen her. With a pretty blush, she bade goodbye to her friends and sauntered over to join me where I sat on the low stone wall.

"All right there?" she asked.

Her voice hitched at the end of the question. It wasn't unusual for girls to respond in that way. Fully aware of my looks, I used my blue eyes to my advantage as often as I could.

"Thinking of going for a drink, but I could be persuaded to skip it."

I lowered my chin, gazing up at her through my eyelashes. In possession of a full arsenal of charming looks, words, touches, and smiles, I rarely relied on more than one at a time, unless it was necessary, of course.

When her cheeks filled with color and her eyes dilated, I knew I had her. Just to be sure, I leaned over and nudged her gently with my shoulder, lingering for a moment to feel the heat of her body through the thin material of my shirt.

"Wh-why would you give the drinks a miss?" Her voice was little more than a whisper.

She pressed her hands into the wall on either side of her hips as though to ground herself. I slowly, deliberately, raked my fingers through my hair, ducking my head as I did so, and then placed my hand on the wall right next to hers. Her little finger twitched, like it wanted to reach out for mine, but she stopped it.

"Why do you think I would skip several hours in a crowded pub, getting stepped on by sweaty people and hit on by girls who aren't nearly so gorgeous as yourself—" I hesitated, savoring each word before I uttered it aloud. "—when I could take you out for a quiet, romantic evening?"

The girl was suddenly coy, staring off in the direction of her friends as though I didn't affect her in the slightest. I pretended not to notice they were all ogling me. Any one of them would have disappeared with me in a heartbeat, but the girl with the most confidence captured my attention. She was no novice, however attractive she found me, and she intended to make me work for my evening of fun. The game was almost more exciting than the reward.

"I don't even know your name." She turned back briefly, but then let her gaze wander off to something over my shoulder.

I stifled a laugh. If she thought she could better resist my advances by not looking at me, she was about to be very surprised. Summoning a hint of my true charm, I focused all my thoughts in her direction.

"Rioghan," I murmured.

Her eyes widened at the sensations I caused, but she had no idea I was the origin. From experience, and lots of it, I knew she felt a low current over her skin, that beautiful, creamy skin, which then intensified somewhere near her heart. This gave her the impression that her reaction was emotional and not physical. That warmth spread throughout her chest and then her belly. Within moments, the girl was convinced she was in love with me—and all because I said my name.

"Rioghan?" She attempted to repeat my name, and then again, slower. "Ree-an."

She was love-drunk by that point and ready for me to take her home. To let her keep the humility to which she'd so desperately clung, I at least asked her name, too.

"Megan."

We did skip the drinks and dinner. There wasn't anything quiet about the night, but there was plenty of romance.

*

Megan was lovely in every way. I brushed a strand of dark hair from her cheek and smiled as she sighed. I hated to wake her, but the day was waiting.

"Good morning, love," I whispered.

Her eyes, an arresting green, fluttered open without recognition, still not awake to memories of the previous night and unfamiliar surroundings. Uncertainty melted into a smile as she focused on my face and stretched her glorious form.

"Hi," she said, her voice husky from sleep. "Is it time to get up?"

"I'm afraid so, beautiful."

"Would you like some breakfast?" She threw the blanket away from her shapely legs.

For a moment, I considered a replay of the previous evening. What a shame the night had to end.

"Just some toast and tea, I think," I said, grabbing my robe.

"It'll be waiting for you."

I didn't miss her longing glance. She grabbed a crisp, white button-down shirt from my closet and pulled it over her tiny vest. I ignored a prickle of irritation at the thoughtless familiarity, because there was something about a woman in a man's shirt.

The smell of strawberries greeted me as I entered the kitchen. I hadn't intended to make breakfast a big affair, but the scent of the fresh berries changed my mind. I lingered longer than usual.

"Would you like to get dinner tonight?" she asked.

I hated to let her down but knew it was necessary. "I can't. I'll be in Cork."

"You don't have a class today?"

I shook my head, and her shoulders dropped. She understood what I didn't say.

While she dressed, I speed-dialed the usual taxi company and then I ushered her out the door and kissed her cheek chastely.

Leaving Dublin hadn't been my intention. Excuses simply eased the transition from lover to stranger. It seemed like an interesting enough way to spend the day, and why shouldn't I? There was no one to answer to and nothing but time.

One beautiful thing about Cork City was that it always thrummed with life, no matter what time of day or night. Even if I was alone, I had thousands of friends and lovers. There was always a gorgeous girl to tease or a guy to talk football with, and then I got to go my merry way, meet another beautiful lass, share a pint with another lady. It never got old, and I never felt lonely.

Since my trip to Cork was spontaneous, I wondered what to do with my day. The forecasted rain had not begun to fall. Though the clouds were oppressive, the weather was still mild enough to sit outside and watch the people that passed. I bought a coffee from O'Brien's and settled on one of the decorative marble benches on Patrick Street. As I sipped, I turned to a fresh page in my journal.

It was strange waking up next to Megan this morning. I know I don't have a type, but if I had to choose, well, a man could do a lot worse than porcelain skin, emerald eyes, and dark curls. And she giggled at my jokes. I like that. It's funny. I don't ask girls to stay. I didn't want to ask her, but...

I frowned, staring blankly at the page.

I can't deny that something feels different. Even if I could share my life with someone, it wouldn't be Megan, or any of my other recent Megans. It doesn't matter. I don't want to be attached anyway.

Sometimes I wonder if Father was right.

Oh, well. Such is life. If I'm stuck here, at least I'm going to have fun. Speaking of fun...

My pen stilled as sweet perfume assailed my senses. Glancing up, I spotted a gorgeous brunette passing with bags from Donovan Cole department store. Her hips swayed under a dangerous miniskirt, and her long legs were encased in leather boots a fraction too tall to be innocent.

As she drew close, I offered a wide, friendly smile. She appeared not to notice, attention fixed firmly on the mobile in her hand, but before passing, her eyes flickered sideways. Sometimes it was too easy to get a girl's attention.

I snapped my journal shut and pitched my coffee in the nearest bin as I followed, putting a bounce in my step and a twinkle in my eye. When she reached the door of Sullivan's Restaurant, I was there in time to hold it for her.

"Good morning," I offered as we passed inside.

She glanced over her shoulder with a doleful expression and then moved to join a lad who waited for her at the bar.

My interest still piqued by the chase, I looked around to see if anyone else might satisfy my tastes. The sounds of conversation and the low clink of silverware filled the air; every table was occupied, and every seat was taken, except the one across from a girl with brilliant red curls.

A mug of tea sat in front of her, and her slender, white hands were folded around it as if to soak up the warmth. In repose, her features were nondescript. There were prettier girls in the bar, but none of them had an empty chair. I approached confidently; getting that seat would be as easy as breathing. Success with Megan the night before made me certain of my persuasive abilities.

"Do you mind if I sit?"

I was met with silence and realized she wore a small set of ear buds. I took the empty seat without an invitation.

She finally looked up and noticed me. Her expression was one of hope, and I realized I'd been too hasty with my initial assessment. The facial features that had been at rest were suddenly alive, causing me to gasp at her extraordinary beauty. I sensed a hint of innocence, something I hadn't seen in a girl's eyes in a long time.

Her grey eyes widened, and that stunning hope turned to irritation. The flash of fury was also lovely, alerting me to the fire inside her.

"What are you listening to?"

With a frown, she pulled the buds from her ears and gave a huge sigh. She resented my intrusion, and I found that amusing. Her scowl deepened.

"Moira Langley," she finally said, naming a very popular opera singer. She then placed her headphones back in, effectively shutting me out.

I snorted in laughter and watched for a few moments more, planning my next attack. "May I hear?"

Her shoulders slumped, and she turned the full force of her glare on me. She didn't seem impressed by my appearance, and that was intriguing. I knew I was handsome; I used that fact to my advantage as often as possible.

She continued to stare, apparently wishing the floor would open and swallow me whole. I dipped my head and peered at her through my eyelashes. That usually did the trick when nothing else worked. The mystery girl was no exception, though she still didn't look happy about it. She ripped the buds out of her ears and shoved the tiny music player across the table.

"Don't put them all the way in your ears," she cautioned. "That's just gross."

I lifted the earphones and held them close enough to hear the voice, making a face as I did so. "Eww. What is that?"

She rolled her eyes and grabbed the device from my hands. "I suppose your taste in music runs the punk or emo route? Or, judging by your appearance, maybe you're missing the boy bands?"

I gasped. "You're American."

"Well spotted." She shut me out once more.

"It's not that I have a problem with the music," I tried again.

I wondered why I worked so hard for her attention. She obviously didn't find me attractive, or if she did, since I couldn't bear to consider the idea that someone might be immune to my baby blues, she had a strange way of showing it. Her eyebrow rose in mock curiosity.

"I love music of all kinds. It's her voice that repulses me."

Her jaw dropped, and she slowly pulled the earpieces away. "How can you say that?"

"It's too brassy, I suppose. Forced, and maybe a bit crude." I was delighted with the way her emotions worked over her face. We were getting somewhere—maybe not where I had originally intended to go, but she was finally talking to me.

"Moira Langley has a glorious voice," she snapped. "Better than Celia Murphy, anyway."

"Oh, believe me. I've been familiar with the human voice for years," I assured her. "While some may find her style appealing, I find it overblown. Wouldn't you rather hear a sweet, clear voice than that?"

"Years?" With a lifted brow and twisted smirk, she shook her head. "How many years could you possibly have studied to believe that you know more than Moira Langley? You can't be older than twenty-one. Your voice hasn't even reached maturity yet."

I didn't try to correct her. Twenty-one was on the high side of what people normally guessed. Instead, I shrugged.

"Perhaps I'm gifted?"

She rolled her eyes, causing me to smirk. "Would you like me to leave?"

I hoped against all hope that her answer was no. I could feel it, though—the yes right on the tip of her tongue. Good manners kicked in, and she reluctantly shook her head.

"No. You can sit here, I guess. I have to leave soon anyway."

We sat, unspeaking, for a full thirty minutes. Since she was so determined to ignore my existence, I took the opportunity to study my surroundings. The first thing that caught my eye was a large man in a suit keeping watch over the girl. I felt a thrill of fear skitter down my spine, but he looked away when he saw I'd noticed him. When I was sure he wasn't going to look again, I resumed my people watching.

People still fascinated me, and I found plenty to write about in my journal. All the petty, useless, mundane events in their tiny little worlds captivated me. For instance, the attractive blonde behind the bar was upset that her boyfriend hadn't taken the rubbish out to the bin the night before. I knew that because I heard her complaining to another lady who was upset that her fifteen-year-old son had been suspended from school for truancy. The man beside her muttered to his companion that those ladies had it easy, because his wife was on the sauce and had a terrible temper when inebriated. His friend was worried about a sound that his car was making and wondered if he had the money to fix it straightaway, or if he would have to press his luck while he saved the cash. What did it *mean* in the grand scheme of things? When their lives were taken as a whole, the seventy or eighty some-odd years that these people were likely to live, how could those things be relevant?

I glanced back at my reluctant companion and saw that she watched me with interest. She wasn't nearly as indifferent as she wanted me to think. I flashed a grin at her, and she glowered in return. That was fine. As long as she didn't mean it, she could scowl, frown, curse, and snipe at me all she wanted.

"You shouldn't listen to people's private conversations, you know," she said suddenly.

She couldn't possibly have known I'd been eavesdropping. Or maybe she could.

"Your face gives you away," she informed me.

"Don't you find them interesting?" I leaned forward with delight, while she wrinkled her nose in disgust.

"Not really."

My eyes narrowed in suspicion. I was sure she had been listening to her beloved opera star, so she couldn't have known what had been said. Before I could even open my mouth, she cut me off.

"What these people have to talk about is none of my business, nor is it any of yours."

My eyes narrowed even further until they were slits through which I regarded her. Her tone told me she found my eavesdropping offensive. She valued her privacy, it seemed. I wanted to deny her that privacy and quiz her for the remainder of the afternoon, but she was back to her music. I wondered if there was a new singer, or if she had a thing for Moira Langley.

Ignoring her silent plea for solitude, I pushed forward with my burning questions. "So, what do you find fascinating?"

"History," she said loudly, talking over the music in her ears.

I chuckled again. Something about her was so enchanting. I certainly knew plenty about history but didn't find it as alluring as she did.

"Why? I mean, it's all gone, like. Whisked away into oblivion, over and done with. I would imagine that the future would hold more enchantment, the mystery of what's to come."

"I didn't think you'd understand. Sometimes there's no mystery about what's to come," she said curtly. She glanced at her watch and stood quickly. "It was nice to meet you."

Her nose wrinkled, leaving me with the impression that perhaps it had not been so nice.

"It was a pleasure to meet you, as well." I looked deeply into her grey eyes as I said the words, hoping she would see I was being completely honest. She rolled those eyes, however, and dashed to the door.

That one girl had me convinced I was losing my touch. I hadn't used the full extent of my charms—sensual touches, pointed gazes, and a hint of the supernatural—but I didn't usually need them. Shrugging, I gathered my things and followed her. I tried not to let it bother me, as I would have eventually had to find a way to let her down easily.

Cork City was a town rich with the history the red-haired girl apparently loved. It was once built on canals, much like Venice. I ducked through an arched doorway that had served as a boat slip hundreds of years before and meandered through a jeans shop. A pretty girl stood at the register, and she noticed me the moment I entered. With a smile, I realized that I had not lost my touch.

"Hello," I said silkily.

She blushed furiously and glanced down at the register. Oh, yes. I still had it—every bit of it.

"Can I help you at all?" the tiny brunette asked.

"Just having a look 'round, if that's okay?"

"Let me know if you see anything you like," she said, then dipped her head in embarrassment at her accidental double entendre.

I chuckled aloud and wandered over to the counter. "I think the prettiest thing here is probably not for sale."

"Yeah?" she whispered, her eyes widening.

"And I doubt that this jumper here would appreciate dinner and dancing, don't you?" I continued, watching carefully for her reaction.

"Oh, absolutely not. Don't waste your time on that jumper." She tossed her dark hair over her shoulder and smiled invitingly.

"Shame, that. I was looking forward to a night out. I don't suppose you'd be interested?"

"Absolutely, I would," she gasped. "I'm off at half-five. You could meet me here?"

"I'll see you then…" I hesitated, waiting for her to tell me her name.

"Anna," she supplied, holding her hand out.

"And I'm Rioghan," I told her. "I'll look forward to it for the rest of the day."

I left the shop, a thrill of anticipation for the evening coursing through me. The sting of my failure with the red-haired girl faded quickly. I had obviously not lost my touch with the ladies, as Anna had proven.

I smiled at another young lady, causing her to flush. She elbowed her friend and nodded in my direction. I chuckled to myself when her friend dropped her bags and stepped right into the middle of them. My confidence was returning quickly. Perhaps I could have mesmerized the girl in the pub with my voice and been done with it? Of course, I could, but where would the fun have been in that?

"Looking lovely today, ladies." I winked and bent to help them salvage their purchases from the rain-slicked sidewalk.

They giggled and covered their blushing cheeks with their hands. It was too easy. I considered finding the red-haired girl again so that she could be a challenging game for me.

I passed a trendy nightclub that was full to capacity, and the smoking patio was spilling over with beautiful people. I stepped inside and joined the revelry easily. By the time I left to meet Anna, I had the number for Melanie. She was a British girl in town for the week, and I promised to give her a ring the next day to make plans.

⸮ ᴆᴏ

I was a master of getting a girl out of my home or hotel room in the morning. I ordered breakfast and talked about getting to work on time. She usually remembered somewhere she had to be as well. It was no different with Anna. She wasn't as pretty in the morning as she had been the night before, but no human ever was.

She accepted the toast and tea gratefully, smiled prettily at me as she asked if she could call sometime, and then waltzed right out the door. I had plenty of uninterrupted time to plan my evening with Melanie, the lovely blonde I had picked up at the nightclub the evening before.

With a spring in my step, I pulled on my jacket and trotted down the steps to the sidewalk. It was a short walk to Oliver Plunkett Street, where several of my favorite pubs were located. Securing a date for the following night might have been overdoing it, but I decided there was no such thing. I peeked through the windows and open doors, searching for the most attractive, tourist-y looking females I could find.

It was essential that the girls I picked up be from other countries, if at all possible. On occasion, I made an exception for an especially pretty girl or, in the case of Anna, to soothe my aching ego. The beauty of visitors, however, was that there would never be talk of a second date. Most importantly, there was never talk of a relationship. The one thing I couldn't risk was getting too close to someone, because there was entirely too much danger in that.

The Benchmark was already full, and live music pumped through the speakers inside. The pub was a great one for the tourists as it offered a great selection of live music and employed rustic décor. I contemplated joining the revelry, but before I could make up my mind, I saw a flash of red-gold and was distracted. Whoever it was had exited a car on The Grand Parade. I hurried forward, wishing I could run without calling undue attention to myself.

It was the girl from Sullivan's Pub, chattering away to a petite blonde woman who stood next to her. How had I missed the fact that the girl was only five feet tall? The older woman had a proud tilt to her head that exactly matched the younger girl's stature when I'd met her the day before. With no further evidence needed, I deduced the women were mother and daughter. The blonde examined the storefront with shrewd eyes, oblivious to the redhead at her side. Without exchanging a word with the younger girl, the woman turned and entered the shop.

The daughter stared after her mother with a dejected frown. Fists clenched at her side in sadness and frustration, she kicked at the ground petulantly before regaining her composure. A mask of indifference fell into place, and she muttered a few words to herself. Before I could approach, she noticed she was alone. Her stony expression slipped into one of fear, and she scrambled to enter the store after her mother.

I wondered if she would appreciate a rescue attempt and was shocked at myself for considering it. Perhaps I would have better luck charming her mother. It would be worth the dirty look the girl was sure to give me. With that decided, I made my way to the front doors. My plan was to creep through the aisles and then try to surprise her. Even if she were shocked, I doubted her face would give anything away.

At the door, I was gobsmacked to see a crowd gathered. The record store was popular, but the amount of people spilling onto the sidewalk seemed excessive. I smiled and winked my way through the throngs, secure in my ability to seem as if I were conferring a great honor upon those whom I shamelessly skipped in line. As far as I was aware, there was only one person alive that would see right through me, and there she was.

She stood next to the blonde, arms crossed and eyes closed. She occasionally let out an exasperated puff of air, but otherwise stood so still that she looked like she'd fallen asleep standing up. I turned to take in her mother and gasped.

Celia Murphy, according to the many posters surrounding her, sat regally behind a poorly disguised card table, more aware of the honor she bestowed upon her subjects than I could ever pretend to be. The girl's deprecating remark about Celia Murphy sprang to mind, and I laughed to myself.

I smiled brightly at a woman who was at the very front of the line, determined to take her spot. She dithered for a moment, so I added a wink and bit my lower lip. She offered to let me cut line. I nodded my thanks graciously and selected a CD from one of the many available piles.

I snuck a quick glance at the girl and realized that her eyes were still closed. Her serenity would be shattered the moment she realized I was there. I didn't know why I was so convinced of her interest in me, since all evidence seemed to point in the opposite direction.

Celia had been watching me with cool interest, perhaps trying to decide if I was someone nearly as important as she. I decided to run with that and grabbed a second CD from a different stack.

"What an honor this is, Ms. Murphy," I said and was rewarded with a glowing smile.

Because I wanted to get my way, I employed the full arsenal of my charms along with my words. Ms. Murphy shifted in her seat, feeling the tingle on her skin inspired by a lover's touch. Her cheeks flushed as she imagined my caress on her neck, my warm breath and a brush of lips. I nipped at her ear and soothed that tiny bite with my tongue. She melted, panting and writhing, and offered herself up to me. Heart pounding, stomach clenching, eyes dilating, she was fully under my spell, and none of it was real except in her mind. From five feet away and without a single movement save for my smile, I seduced her fully.

The girl's eyes snapped open and glared at me. While the older woman was ready to crawl across the table for my tall form, broad shoulders, full lips, and sculpted cheekbones, the younger one looked ready to eviscerate me. I was dismayed to see that I had been correct about the effect the shirt would have on her eyes. They were a devastating silver, made even more startling by the flash of anger in them.

"What are you doing here?" she hissed.

Celia turned and frowned at her daughter before attempting to dazzle me with her smile. Though she was completely under my spell, I allowed her to believe the situation was reversed. She believed me to be fully captivated.

"If you don't mind signing two, I would appreciate it. My father is a big fan, but he was held up in a very important meeting." I slid both albums toward her waiting pen.

"Of course not…" She trailed off, waiting for me to supply my name.

"Rioghan." I spelled it for her.

"What an interesting name. Does it have a meaning?" Her eyes sought mine, and I knew that, with some persuasion, the truth would be believed in the most literal sense of the words.

"Little King." I winked.

"And the Big King?" Her eyes were wide with wonder.

"I'm afraid I'm not at liberty to say," I whispered, as if we were the only two involved in a very important secret.

"Of course," she breathed. "I'll just sign my name then?"

"I do wonder, though," I began, feigning embarrassment.

She nodded encouragingly.

"Well, I wondered if your daughter might be able to come with me and meet my father. He is one of your biggest fans. I can see you are far too busy to make a special visit, but I know he would be thrilled to make her acquaintance."

I didn't dare look at the girl as I said this. Part of me wished for hope on her face, but another part was well aware that there might be hatred. I focused instead on maintaining the connection with her mother, mentally encouraging her to acquiesce without asking too many questions.

"Absolutely," Celia crowed. "And please thank the king—I mean, your father. I hope I will have the honor of meeting him soon, as well."

After getting the answer I desired, I turned off the charm like a light switch. Suddenly, Celia was the most important person in her own world again. She waved her daughter around the table like a servant and addressed the next person in line.

I moved my gaze to the newly freed captive. She stared at me in disbelief, her movements jerky and almost clumsy as I led her through the crush of people. We reached the sidewalk, and I took a deep breath of cleansing air while those wide, silver eyes continued to search my face.

"Why? How?" she started. The shock of her liberty had still not worn off.

"You looked miserable," I told her.

"Ugh. Crap. Celia hates it when I look miserable at these stupid things," she muttered.

"Well, it was hard to tell." I tried to comfort her. "Your eyes were closed."

"Why would you rescue me? How did you manage to completely dumbfound my mother? She never lets me out of these stupid signings." Her shoe found a stone on the walk, and she kicked it viciously.

"As I said, love, you looked truly miserable. And dealing with your mother was very easy. She wants to believe that the very best and brightest come to see her. I merely played on that desire."

I had thrown some of the old "Rioghan Hypnosis" in for good measure, just to be sure.

"You're not some prince?" Her question was loaded with accusations.

"Not as she believes me to be, no."

My most charming, toothy smile went unrewarded. I considered laying on the charm, but she turned away and flagged a taxi.

"Well, thanks for springing me. I'll be on my way, then."

Without another word, she ducked into the waiting taxi and slammed the door before I could even move.

I stared after the car with my mouth hanging open, appalled at her lack of gratitude. The girl was incorrigible. I wanted to never think of her again, but I no doubt would. Eternity on this rock, and all I could concentrate on was one rather nondescript girl who, to that point, had thwarted my every advance.

As a result of my distraction, the evening with Melanie did not go as well as I had hoped. She was quite beautiful, an ethereal blonde with luminous green eyes. I believed she was witty and intelligent, but I honestly couldn't remember one word of the conversation that we had.

I ended the night without extending my usual invitation for a nightcap at my place. I knew Melanie was disappointed, but I honestly didn't think I would be able to focus on her. Instead, I paid her taxi fare and left her with a soft kiss to the cheek.

When her cab was out of sight, I ducked into the alley and vanished. I arrived at my home and spent the evening by an unnecessary hearth-fire, pondering the mystery of the red-haired girl in the pages of my journal.

The girl with the red hair. Something about her truly grabs me. She's not sweet; she's not drawn to me. She has a wicked tongue that makes me laugh. I suppose I should be offended, but instead I'm intrigued.

She seems to have a similar relationship with her mother as I have with Father. She even calls her mother by her first name. This blatant disregard baffles me and amuses me at the same time. Imagine if I were to call Father Ailbhe. I don't think I'd live to tell about it.

There's no point in dwelling, I know. There will always be a part of me that wonders what defenses she employs against me and why. Ireland, though small, is home to many people. I doubt I'll see her again and if I should, my doubt is stronger that she would have changed her attitude toward me.

Closing the leather-bound book, I decided that, if I met her again, I would ignore her as fully and as effectively as she seemed to ignore me. She had ruined my night already; I would not allow her to ruin any more of my trysts.

JENNIFER M. BARRY

A TRI

I watched the couple in front of me with barely disguised interest. Whatever they were arguing about was minor, but their expressions told me that they believed it to be the end of the world. Shaking my head, I contemplated the problems that could possibly cause such turmoil in an obviously loving relationship. Money, employment, family, fear of commitment? It all seemed pretty minor to me when love hung in the balance. Shouldn't that have been the deciding factor? If they loved each other, couldn't they put everything else aside and just love?

I had plenty of experience using my powers to convince women that they loved *me*, but there in that little coffee shop, I considered covering the arguing couple with a charm that would re-ignite their passion for one another. Sipping my latte in an overly casual fashion, I moved closer to their table to maximize my intended effect. I also wanted to eavesdrop. No one could judge me for that.

The girl leaned over the table with her right hand knotted into her hair at her temple. The boy was relaxed, seemingly at ease with the whole discussion. Perhaps he believed her to be over-reacting. Maybe he didn't care as much about the argument as she did, or the relationship simply was not as important to him as it was to her. I watched for another moment, unable to hear what they were murmuring.

"My mother does not hate you."

Agitation boosted the boy's volume, and I could finally hear the conversation clearly. The girl answered loudly, too, her tone simmering just below a yell.

"She's always making these veiled compliments like, 'What a lovely shirt. Don't I wish I had a figure to wear something that low cut?' and 'Perhaps you should try to get more water into your diet and cut out those fizzy drinks, love,' and 'Isn't your mother holy, love?' What could she possibly *mean* by that? She thinks I'm a fat slapper with shite parents."

"She's complimenting you. And that other one is because she cares about you. To her, a healthy diet and regular Mass are important. She can't help it, really," the boy pleaded.

His grin was still firmly in place, telling me he found the whole argument completely absurd. Of course it would be more important to her than to him.

I concentrated for a moment and sent out the first wave. The couple barely moved, but I knew it hit them because the girl's eyes widened and her cheeks flushed.

"I don't know how she managed to raise such a nice guy." She leaned over the table and licked her bottom lip slowly.

"I've not always been like this. You bring out the better parts of me." He gazed at her through lowered eyelids.

I chuckled. They truly did love each other. With another concerted effort, I sent the spell again.

"If you don't stop being so nice, I'll have to forgive her for everything," the girl murmured with a giggle.

"I like the low-cut shirt." The boy waggled his eyebrows.

She blushed and ran a hand through her brunette waves, smoothing out the knots from her earlier ministrations.

"I think you should buy more of them, in fact. Maybe we'll drop by Douglas Court on the way home and get some for you."

The girl leaned forward even more and touched his knee underneath the table. He shifted slightly and reached for her free hand.

"I think we should go home now and skip the shopping," she said in a husky voice. He dropped her hand immediately and tossed back the rest of his coffee.

"I have no argument for that." He laughed, dragging her from her chair and pulling her into a tight embrace. "I love you so much, Katie."

"I love you, too, Donal. We'll not worry what our families say, yeah?"

They kissed fiercely, and I smiled, feeling my work had been done. It was a balm to the soul to see two people changed by each other. Change was not something with which I was familiar, so I enjoyed being a part of it anytime I could.

"Ah, get a room," someone called from the corner.

Katie buried her head in Donal's chest and giggled. He grinned shyly into her hair before grabbing her hand and dragging her out of the café.

With my first subjects gone, I cast about the little shop for another project. The first had been such a success that I wanted to see what else I could get into. A girl in the corner was staring at the cashier. I gazed at him appraisingly, wondering what it was she found so attractive. His hair stuck up all over his head, and the tips were blue. The tattoos on his arms and neck were excessive, but when he smiled at a customer, I could hear that poor girl in the corner sigh.

I turned my attention to her, taking in her messy, honey-blonde ponytail and scrubbed-clean face. Her glasses were trendy, but she would have been more attractive without them, because a pair of warm brown eyes sparkled behind the lenses. Her jumper hung on her frame, and I could see that she was athletic, probably on a girls' football team. It had the potential for a good match, but they couldn't know if they weren't given the chance to explore the possibility.

I sent the first wave of lust as the cashier looked toward the corner. It was easier if they were looking at the object of the experiment when the charm was cast. He froze as his eyes rested on the girl, and he shook his head slowly, wondering what that sudden attraction was. The girl looked up, caught his eye, and dropped her biscuit into her coffee. The hot liquid splashed onto her shirt, and she moaned in abject mortification. Cashier-boy dropped the change he was counting and slammed the register shut. In a flash, he grabbed a towel and made his way to her side.

"Thanks very much." She swiped at her jumper and laughed self-consciously when the stains remained.

"I'm Brendan," the cashier said.

"Michelle." She took his offered hand.

"I'd offer to buy you a coffee, but," he started.

"I'm dangerous with it?" She laughed as she finished his sentence.

"Maybe a movie instead?"

I grinned in triumph. I was pretty good at pairing couples. Of course, there was already someone else with the distinction of being the supernatural matchmaker, but it was fun to play around sometimes. At least I tried to make sure the subjects were suited to each other. Cupid would match a baboon to a horse if inter-species mating were possible, just for the laugh. If he were in a truly terrible mood, he would wreak havoc among even the most stable of marriages. He was definitely not someone to piss off, in any case.

I left the coffee house and walked down St. Patrick's Street, lost in thought. Love was something that had managed to elude me for the whole of my existence. Seeing it in action thrilled me but baffled me beyond words. I loved my father, even if we frequently disagreed on how I should behave. I loved my mother and knew she thought of me often. Romantic love crossed my mind on many occasions. I delighted in female company, of course, but that was all I ever allowed myself. Maybe I had been missing something. Where was the conversation, the comfortable silence, the solace of knowing that one person accepted me for what I was? I hurried to hold the door for a lady who was laden with purchases and felt my confidence return with her look of awe.

She was quite pretty, with curling chestnut hair and warm, brown eyes. I spoke before I could think. "Could I buy you a coffee?"

Never mind that I had just come from the coffee house.

"Really?" she breathed, her face turning a tantalizing shake of pink. "I'd love one."

Her reply came out more as a gasp, and it bolstered my already enormous ego. I held my hand out to take her bags from her. Who needed prickly, short, ungrateful, slightly plain, strawberry blonde, deep-thinking girls? I certainly didn't, not with such a lovely, if slightly vapid, lady in front of me.

"Right, then." I swept her back out the door and down the sidewalk.

She walked quickly to keep up with me, her wool coat swishing with her steps. I glanced at her appraisingly, liking the flush that still colored her cheeks and the long, slender legs encased in jeans and heeled boots. She was eyeing me, too, like all her birthdays had come at once. I shook my head and chuckled.

The spiky-haired cashier wasn't surprised to see me again. He still stared at the girl in the corner, a smile playing on his lips. She looked up at him shyly, and I was thrilled to see that my spell remained firmly in place. Brendan handed over my white coffee and a caramel-chocolate-whipped-cream-and-sprinkles filled thing for my companion. I hadn't even asked her name. Maybe it was time to try a bit of the conversation that had been eluding me.

"I'm Rioghan, by the way," I said with a laugh.

She giggled into her coffee and licked the whipped cream off her top lip.

"That's embarrassing," she murmured, swiping at her face with a napkin. "I'm Emma. Thanks very much for the coffee."

"You're most welcome."

Goosebumps swept from her jaw to her shoulder, a response to the sensation of my warm breath on her neck and the nip of my teeth at her ear. She flushed and bowed her head, covering her flaming cheeks with a curtain of soft brown hair. I mentally kicked myself. We couldn't exchange stimulating words if I kept her tongue tied with my supernatural seduction. I eased the spell and was rewarded when she looked me in the eyes with confidence again.

We fell silent as I tried to think of something to talk about. The things I would normally say in that situation were designed solely to get her back to my home or hotel room. I found myself clueless with a woman for the second time that week.

She stared at me, her eyes bright with barely hidden want as she busied herself with stirring her coffee.

"Are you from the city?" she finally asked, clearly deciding that I was not going to break the silence.

"I'm actually from Cratloe." I named a tiny town as far removed from city-life as possible. She frowned, so I decided to tease her. "You seem disappointed."

"You do seem like a city boy," she explained, shifting nervously. "I'm from Bantry. I moved to the city to do some modeling work. There's so much more to do here. I like to go to the nightclubs most nights to see what I can get into. You should join me sometime."

Her offer was accompanied by a pretty smile, but I was already zoning out on her. She was exactly the kind of girl I always looked for, but I suddenly wanted much, much more.

"What was the last book you read?" I asked.

She looked up in surprise, forgetting to remove the cream from her lips. She had to search for her answer, so I knew it wouldn't be interesting in the least. I handed her a napkin and indicated where she should use it.

"I mostly read magazines," she admitted.

She then named a popular Irish author, but it was phrased more as a question than a statement, like she hoped for my approval. I nodded, though I didn't consider that author's work literature.

"Compelling reads," I noted.

She smiled and leaned back, believing me to be satisfied with her intellect. I was only getting started.

"You like dancing, then?" I asked.

She nodded, her hair swinging invitingly. She was so pretty.

"What's your favorite kind of music?"

"I like a little of everything, I suppose." She named a few pop stars and a rock band. I made a conscious effort not to roll my eyes. "I'm not a symphony girl, if you know what I mean."

"I do," I assured her, adding *unfortunately* inside my head. "No waltzes for you, is that it?"

"Definitely." Her eyes twinkled. "I'm a fun-loving girl, not a snooze-fest."

Stop trying so hard, I wanted to scream. Oh, to find an attractive girl with the wisdom of the ages and the ability to still have fun. Were there none who existed? *Red-haired girl*, my mind whispered. I shook off the thought and tried once more.

"Do you get to travel?"

"I haven't much." She twirled a strand of her hair in a way that I'm sure she believed was inviting. "I'd love to someday model in Paris or Milan, though."

"Oh, dear," I said with exaggerated politeness and glanced at my watch. "I'm afraid I've left someone stranded. Please accept my apology. I'm so very sorry to be rude."

Well, I *was* sorry to be rude, but I couldn't handle any more. I cast a quick charm over her to cushion the blow. She gave me a dazed smile. So pretty. Damn that red-haired girl.

"Not a bother," she said absently. "Thanks very much for the coffee and the conversation."

"The pleasure has been mine." I took her hand and gave her knuckles a quick buss.

She visibly melted, nearly whimpering as I pulled away. I feared I had used entirely too much charisma, but I didn't worry myself with that. I needed an escape, and quickly. Would I forever compare everyone I met to the red-haired girl? What was the hold she had over me? I ran for the door, found the first empty alley possible, and took my leave of the city before I could be spotted.

a ceathair

Though I had seen many corners of the Earth, I considered Ireland my home since my first glimpse of her. The rolling verdant hills held a magic to which even I could not compare. Though the rain came often, I took comfort in it and did not feel disappointment. The sun was no stranger to Ireland; indeed, when it shone upon the lush, muted green, turning it to sparkling emerald, I found it a close friend. The rain was where her secrets lay. The clouds and mist wrapped themselves seductively around the ancient stone walls of castles long since deserted. Fog rolled over the waters of the River Shannon, creeping eerily over the banks and bringing with it a chill that sparked the imagination. The land held mysteries I felt no compulsion to solve.

There was a mystery that *did* tug at my mind, however, and would not release me. From my seat high atop the castle ruins in Cratloe, I stared out over the checkerboard fields below. The girl was a fixture in my thoughts so often that when I saw her approaching through the tall grass at the base of the ruins, I believed her to be a mirage. Surely she was only a figment of my imagination. Moving with dancing steps, she held her arms wide as if to embrace the scene before her.

I tried to view it all through her eyes, which had never before seen the beautiful, flourishing Irish countryside. She'd mentioned her regard for the past, and from that little I knew of her, I imagined she was playing the history of that very patch of land through her mind. Her eyes were wide, taking in the low, velvet slopes, and puzzle pieces separated by crumbling rock walls that had somehow stood the test of time. My eyes clenched shut as visions of the past came flowing back to me in flashes. Untouched Ireland, not yet named and long before any human foot had ever walked the rich grass of the hills.

My ancestors dancing gaily without fear of discovery. The druids with their terrifying rituals, shedding blood to the ground in sacrifice. St. Patrick bringing the message of Christ to a barbaric people. The Celts, angry and righteous, spilling yet more life into the ancient soil to protect that which they deemed rightfully theirs. The arrogant British rulers who claimed a wild and beautiful land as their own.

I wondered if she thought the same things as she touched timeworn stone with a respectful hand.

She had her ever-present music and danced along to a melody that I could not hear. Weak light filtered through clouds that were not threatening, merely comforting, and caressed the spun gold of her hair. She had tied it up, but the curls wouldn't be bound. Her cheeks were flushed, from excitement or the sun, I didn't know. She seemed to revel in her freedom, happy to be unchained. The picture before me was very different to the scared girl I'd seen outside the record store. Perhaps the crush of people in the city had dampened her joy, while wide-open spaces magnified it.

She arrested me fully. I was shackled, and I couldn't fathom what fascinated me about her. Surely her temper and sense of superiority should have made her less attractive to me, but I found them refreshing. Her lack of interest was something of a conundrum, as well. The girl had worked actively to discourage me. Perhaps it was the thrill of the chase? I would discover what her weakness was, and then she would be mine for the taking. Once I conquered that feisty wisp of a girl, the game would be over and I could finally turn my thoughts to other activities.

Just as I made the decision to toy with an innocent girl's emotions, I felt the world stop spinning. The wind stilled, the babbling brook was silenced, and neither bird nor insect offered their song. But there was music. Oh, God above, the most glorious music I had ever heard. The voice was sweeter than any flower in creation, stronger than the stones that supported me, and clearer than the very air I breathed. I couldn't liken it to anything; a pealing bell would have been crude in comparison. Her song was why the brook no longer danced and the birds no longer warbled their tune. Were they perhaps as enamored as I, or were they feeling the first rush of jealousy?

The song abruptly changed, and while it was still beautiful, a bone-chilling sadness colored the words. She stepped over the threshold of the castle ruins, and the sweet notes rang throughout the cavernous stone structure.

The stage she set was clear in my mind: trees bare in the dead of winter, covered in sparkling ice that, while beautiful, was also cold and unyielding. An empty house with dusty windows that filtered the sunless light across a naked stone floor. A hearth with long-dormant coals that hadn't seen fire in years.

Despair the song was designed to evoke filled me, but the instrument was the reason for the emotion. Her voice encompassed me in a rush of silk as she cried out for her lover to return. With a start of shock, I touched my cheek and found it was wet with tears. I couldn't remember the last time I had cried—possibly never.

My body moved of its own accord, pulling me toward the girl with the flame-colored hair. She would be less than thrilled to see me, to know that I had intruded upon her private moment, but I couldn't stop. I descended the stairs with care, not for my own safety, but to keep my presence a secret for as long as possible. I imagined the flash of irritation in her eyes, the frown on her lips when she discovered me, yet I couldn't still my movements. I glided over the ancient rubble, her song pulling me like a magnet until she came into view.

She sat on a rock that had fallen from the medieval walls, facing an opening that once served as a window. A sad smile touched her mouth as she gave life to the final words of the song, *Turn bleak December once more into May.*

"It's beautiful." I breathed, my pulse racing. She jumped up with wild eyes and backed herself against the wall. "No. Please don't be afraid. I didn't want to disturb you, but I couldn't help myself. Your voice, it's... I've never heard anything..."

"Talk much?" She scowled, but the expression was so fleeting, I almost missed it. She didn't exactly appear contrite, but she did seem apologetic.

My heart returned to its normal pace with her words, and a laugh bubbled over.

"What are you doing here?" She glared at me, wearing the exact expression I had expected.

"I'm afraid I was here first. You seem to have stumbled upon my favorite thinking spot." I strolled toward her, pressing my luck even further. "It is beautiful, you know."

"Please, stop," she begged. "I didn't want anyone to hear me."

The grin slid from my face, and I held up my hands with palms toward her, as if warding her off.

"I'm very sorry. I'll leave you alone now." I turned and walked toward the exit quickly, not wanting to make her angrier.

"Wait."

Her voice was strained. It had taken all of her strength to utter the word. I paused, raising an eyebrow, but I didn't turn.

"I'm sorry. That was rude. Thank you. I'm Lily, by the way. If we're going to keep running into each other, you might as well know my name."

"Was that so hard?" I asked, chancing a brief glance over my shoulder.

Hurt and embarrassment etched her face. I turned to face her, to comfort, but she waved me away.

"Do you live around here?" Her voice was brighter and might have fooled me if I hadn't seen her pain.

It was a feeble attempt to change the subject, but I was so pleased with her attention that I answered readily. "I live in a few different places. Well, I guess my permanent home is near Dublin. I'm here most of the time, but I like to travel as often as I can. I have a place in Dublin City and one in London, for when I crave the city lights."

She shook her head in wonder. "Who are you?"

"Oh, I'm sorry. I'm Rioghan." I held my hand out to shake hers.

"No. I mean, you're barely older than I am, but you have a place in Dublin? Are you a trust fund baby?"

I chuckled at her ill-informed assumption that I was even close to her age as my mind formed an answer that would satisfy her. "If that means do I come from a wealthy family, then yes."

"Maybe we're really not so different, but then no one seems to be normal anymore. I get mad sometimes because my father's never been around and my mom usually doesn't remember I'm alive. I mean, she does, because she makes sure I eat and that I stay safe. She cares if my tutors are pleased with my performance and my voice coach says I'm working hard…"

She seemed lost in her own thoughts, unaware that she spoke aloud.

"But none of it seems normal. I took my final exams in a hotel room while other girls got ready for the prom. It's ridiculous to feel like I've missed out, since I was in Tokyo or Paris when everyone else was at pep rallies, but…" She trailed off, and I noticed with a twisting pain in my chest that she was crying.

"Oh, please don't cry," I begged. Prickly Lily was hard to resist, but Sad Lily broke down every last defense I had.

"I'm not crying," she insisted, dragging the back of her hand across her eyes. "Okay, I am. I know it's stupid. I've got it easy, don't I? All the money I want, a new city every week, people doing whatever I tell them to do... I'm the princess who hates her kingdom."

Her words stabbed me to the deepest parts of my heart. We were *exactly* alike, in so many ways that I couldn't even begin to tell her. I stood in her shoes, and had for thousands of years. What was all of it without love? Would I have been more inclined to ascend to the throne if my father had given it with compassion instead of resentment? Would I have had more regard for my own people if their leader, the king, had shown me one ounce of love over the previous centuries?

In the wake of my stunned silence, her mask dropped again. Determined Lily was as precious as the previous two Lilys I had already seen. She turned to exit the castle, and I followed her.

"So what part of America are you from?" I asked, wondering if she would welcome or resent the change in subject. She answered so quickly that I knew it was the former.

"Everywhere." Her eyes rolled. "I suppose I call New York my real home, but I don't spend any more time there than anywhere else."

"I've never been to America," I told her, the sudden realization hitting me. "I have family there, I think."

"You having family strikes me as weird." Lily laughed at my puzzled frown.

I was thrilled to hear her laughter, which sounded so much like her singing, but still stung by her comment. I had to ask her what she meant.

"I don't know. You strike me as a loner. It's kind of freaky to think of you sitting down to dinner with a mom and a dad." She kicked at a stone and watched it sail through the air to land with a small thud somewhere out of sight in the tall grass.

"We don't get along very well," I admitted.

"Do you annoy the piss out of them, too?" she asked, her smile firmly in place. The smile wasn't real, but it was practiced and would convince most people.

"More like a lifestyle difference."

"Oh." Shock contorted her features. Her shoulders relaxed, and I wondered what she'd found comforting about my words. Maybe she had discovered some point of solidarity between the two of us.

We walked through the familiar fields of my homeland and soon entered the little village of Cratloe. She was content to walk next to me and even made polite conversation as we searched through some of the little shops.

"I love Irish chocolate," she muttered as she handed over some change for a packet of Malteasers.

I chuckled at the sounds of enjoyment she made over the candy and wondered what had changed her attitude so fully. I hadn't used any of my actual powers on her, though I had certainly considered it. After a few more moments of fruitless thought, I decided to either give up or ask her what suddenly made her so companionable. Worried that I might hurt her feelings with the latter decision, I let the subject drop. When she offered me a handful of her sweets, I knew I had made the right choice.

She led me next to a small knit shop and dragged me inside enthusiastically. She muttered something about a fisherman's sweater and how Celia would hate it. My eyes to wandered through the tiny aisles as she chattered. It was amusingly quaint, with worn wooden boards below our feet and wavy glass in the window that had certainly been there since the store was first built. Apparently, the pub in town was far enough away that no drunkards could toss each other through the storefront on their way home.

"How random that you were in that castle," she said out of the blue. She held up an Irish knit sweater and examining the price. "I saw it from the bus on the way into town and knew I had to sing there. I get lost in my imagination in places like that, you know? I pictured Ireland before that castle even stood. Back when the druids were doing their crazy rituals, and when St. Patrick came and tried to sell Christianity."

She had obviously been thinking the very things that I had thought. How different her imagination was to the reality. I suddenly wished that I could show her, share my own memories of a wild and bloody Ireland. I shook off the desire, knowing I would send her screaming if I were to use my gifts. Instead, I smiled my most understanding smile and wordlessly encouraged her to continue.

"I think I'll buy this," she decided.

The sweater was a deep blue that brought out the roses in her cheeks and darkened her eyes to a mysterious pewter. I nodded my agreement and watched her go to pay. I waited patiently as she had a brief conversation with the shopkeeper, but was too far away to hear what was said. When she turned, her smile faded into such sadness that it took my breath.

"Everyone bloody knows who I am," she sighed, grabbing my arm and dragging me from the store. "I know it's inevitable, especially as famous as my mother is, but sometimes I just want to be invisible. It even gets scary when I'm by myself and people recognize me, but that lady was nice enough."

I didn't know how to reply, so I wordlessly followed her to the bus stop.

"I have to go on to Galway," she announced, plopping down on a bench.

"Sure," I agreed.

"You're coming, too?" she asked.

I shrugged. "Why not?"

She heaved a great sigh and leaned back against the glass of the bus stop.

The sky above us had been blue for most of the morning, but clouds were beginning to gather. June in Ireland is quite warm, but the weather could change very easily. She looked indifferent at the thought of possible rain, and she had her new sweater should the temperature drop. I didn't worry about her comfort for the moment and, instead, sat as far from her as possible.

"You don't like it when people know you?" I asked quietly.

She stared in the opposite direction, and I knew that she was going to completely ignore my question. I was shocked when she took a deep breath and spoke.

"I just want to be normal."

"Haven't we all felt that way before? I wish that all the time," I assured her.

She gave me an appraising look and nodded. "I imagine you do."

Again, I frowned. She accepted that easily enough. What did she think was so strange or different about me? After years of observing human behavior, I was pretty sure that I had the act down. Before I could let it truly consume me, the bus arrived, so I stood to follow her.

"You don't have anything better to do?" Indignation colored her voice.

"Galway is always beautiful in June." I nudged her up the steps.

She dug through her pocket and came back with a few coins, but I waved her hand away and paid her fare. She looked like she wanted to object, but then sighed again and took a seat. The sighs would have to stop. They were entirely too frequent and broke my heart each time I heard one.

"Howr'ya." A small voice greeted us as we were getting settled. Lily turned and grinned at the boy behind her. "You're gorgeous, ye know that? Is he your boyfriend, like?"

"Emphatically no," Lily said with a laugh.

"Well what's he doing with you then, following you around like a lost dog?" the boy pressed.

"I've wondered the same thing." She eyed me slyly. I pulled an affronted expression, and it made her giggle. "What's your name?"

"I'm Ciarán," he announced proudly. "I'd be proud to be your fellow, you know? Can I take ye to the cinema?"

"How old are you?" I interrupted.

"I'm nine and a half." He puffed out his chest. "What's it to ye?"

The saucy pup was going to get a black eye; I could feel it.

"I'm twice your age." Lily gasped, tears of laughter coming to her eyes.

"Doesn't matter, love. I'm very experienced." He nodded sagely, causing Lily to laugh even harder.

Even I had to chuckle at that. The little chancer kicked my seat, narrowly missing my leg.

"Why aren't you in school?" I asked brusquely.

"Summer holidays, ya eejit." He rolled his eyes toward Lily. "He's a thick one, in'e?"

The cub was begging for a clatter.

"Oh, he's not a total loss, really." Lily came to my defense.

Why my heart should soar with her words, I couldn't know. Surely I didn't see this chubby, freckle-faced *boy* as some kind of rival? However, he made Lily truly laugh, a feat that I had yet to accomplish.

"I'm old enough to go to another city by meself," Ciarán said. "I'm, eh, I'm visiting me big brother at the university. They had to go back to school last week for summer term."

He looked chuffed, either because he had a brother in college or because he wasn't required to attend class while his brother was. Perhaps it was having the undivided attention of the copper-haired girl in our company.

"So how about that movie?" he said, winking.

Lily turned her incredulous eyes on me, and I shrugged. She begged me wordlessly for something to say. I bit my lip to keep from laughing out loud.

"I could chaperone," I offered and received a swift kick to the shin for my efforts.

My eyes watered, and I glowered at the boy in tatty jeans. His t-shirt clung to his round belly like second skin. For a brief moment, I felt a surge of sympathy for him.

"You're very kind," Lily said gently. "I'm afraid that my mother has me very busy while I'm here. Perhaps when you're eighteen you might look me up?"

Ciarán straightened in his chair importantly and nodded. "I'll see you before then, though," he promised.

Lily laughed out loud. It was contagious, and I joined her readily. Ciarán stared at us both as if we'd lost our minds before grinning. Poor little guy didn't even have all of his adult teeth yet. Where did he find such confidence?

"So what do you do all day? It must get boring being by yourself all the time during the summer. Do you read a lot?"

The boy snorted and shook his head. "Football. Stare at girls. More football."

"But books are way more exciting than that. It's not just learning, which can be boring, I'll give you that. Reading lets you go to other places, to escape where you are and enter different worlds. Well, the learning part is important, too."

Ciarán stared at Lily in horror before bursting into laughter. "Hey, Red, you don't look a thing like me ma!"

Lily laughed and shook her head. "I know, I know. You just seem like a smart kid. I thought you might like some of the books I like; that's all."

Caring Lily. How many Lilys were there? From the look in those beautiful grey eyes of hers, she cared about the annoying little twit. Unfortunately, her concern only served to make Ciarán more sure of himself, if that was possible.

"Oh, I read plenty. Don't you worry about that. Let's talk about you. Are ye famous at all?" His eyes flitted back and forth between us.

I knew that wasn't a new question for Lily, and I tensed for her response.

"Not at all," she said lightly, and I sighed in relief.

"You both look it." He appraised us openly. "You're too beautiful to be real, like. I thought ye might be movie stars."

"We're both completely normal people," she insisted. "And besides, I'm sure I look utterly plain next to Rioghan, here."

She nudged me lightly with her elbow, but I didn't have the chance to revel in the fact that she was insinuating that I was beautiful.

Ciarán's eyes narrowed at the mention of my name. I experienced a moment of panic as I wondered if he was a believer of legends, or maybe if he'd only heard them. In any case, he knew the name.

"Like Prince Rioghan?" he asked disdainfully. "Your parents named you after that—"

"Yes." I cut off whatever else he might have said.

He did know the legends. That could get sticky.

"Stupid name," Ciarán said, kicking my seat again.

The urge to introduce his face to my fist returned with vengeance.

"I think it's a beautiful name," Lily said gently. "As is the name Ciarán."

The boy and I were both mollified, and I rethought violence. He was only a child, after all. She thought I was beautiful and with no help from my special skills. The knowledge sank in, and I felt like singing. I turned to face the window and watched the scenery flash by in a blur of green and grey. The rain that had threatened finally fell, and I cursed myself for not thinking to bring an umbrella. Well, it was an impromptu trip, after all, inspired by Lily.

She and Ciarán continued to converse. He asked questions about America, and she gently spurned his childish advances. I listened with one ear as she described New York City, the skyscrapers, the crush of people, the yellow taxi cabs, the trains, the tree at Rockefeller Center when it was lit up at Christmas, and the phenomenal food. He seemed as amazed by that magical place that she described as I was.

By the time we reached Galway, little Ciarán was so utterly taken with Lily that he didn't want to leave her side.

"You'll come see me and my brother at the university?" he asked, pulling her toward a taxi rank.

"I can't, love," she said, easily slipping into the Irish dialect. "My mother is waiting for me. We have a stupid meeting this evening, and if I'm late she'll kill me."

"Ah, you're an adult, aren't you?" He stomped his foot impatiently. "Tell her to kiss—"

"Easier said than done. But we will see you again, okay?" she said.

"Right, so. Lily, it's been a pleasure." He lifted her hand and kissed it, as he believed a gentleman should do. "Rioghan, your name is still stupid."

With that, he jumped into the cab and slammed the door.

"What on earth?" Lily cried, turning to me with tears of laughter in her eyes. "He was a mess, wasn't he?"

I was scowling darkly at the back window of the motoring taxi and had to remind myself that he was only a child.

JENNIFER M. BARRY

À CUIG

"Hello, Rioghan." A voice interrupted my stealthy entrance.

"Father." My acknowledgment was terse.

"You've been mingling with commoners more than usual lately," he said, his gaze boring into my back.

I turned in resignation.

"You know I like them." I crossed my eyes in a juvenile expression of irritation and let out an exasperated huff.

"Hmmm, yes. But I wonder if there's something that draws you now, more so than ever?" he questioned silkily.

"I don't see how it concerns you," I retorted, turning once more toward my chambers.

"You'd want to be more careful in your manner of speaking," Father said, a hint of anger creeping into his otherwise smooth voice. "Morrigan has been asking after you."

"Yes, my master. How is Auntie Morrigan, anyway? Vile as ever, I'm sure."

Before he could formulate his next words, I disappeared down the long hallway. After spending the day in the Cratloe ruins, our own castle seemed too bright, too perfect. The walls of stone were perfectly maintained, the chandeliers in pristine condition. I stole over the ancient woven rugs that showed no sign of wear or tear, glowering at paintings of my father that had been gifts from artistic masters through the ages.

I studied the images of Ailbhe, or rather, others' interpretations of him. He was beautiful, with classic features, a wide forehead, sculpted cheekbones, a square jaw, and piercing blue eyes. Black hair waved to his shoulders, no matter what the style of the era. He had never concerned himself with what humans found attractive, though any woman who ever laid eyes on him would have been under his spell immediately. What did interest me were the changes in his expressions throughout the years. Once loving, animated, and generous, his face appeared in later paintings to have harder planes. His mouth was pinched and set into a narrow line, and his eyes, no longer open and full of care, had become shrewd and calculating. It pained me these glorious works by Degas, Da Vinci, and Van Gogh, among others, would never see the light of day. They were effectively entombed in a virtual mausoleum.

I hated my home. After breathing the beautiful, clean air of Cratloe and wandering the crowded streets of Galway, I felt suffocated. My chambers had been designed to my exact specifications, but the rooms brought me no comfort. The enormous feather bed gave no invitation. The mirror over the bureau reflected a wistful face with sad eyes. When had my sheltered life ceased to be enough?

"I'll be staying in Cork for a while," I announced to no one in particular.

With the hundreds of servants lurking throughout the castle, perhaps even in the room with me, my father would get the message. I began throwing clothes and other essentials into a large case. After a moment of deliberation, I grabbed a second case and filled it, too. I nodded with satisfaction when I realized that I would have no reason to return to this veritable dungeon for a long while. Stopping only once more on my way out, I grabbed some currency from a small safe behind the painting of my mother.

How does one paint an angel? It couldn't be done, not without taking away much of the original glory. They didn't have corporeal forms unless they were visiting Earth, which didn't happen as often as one might think. Instead, they were a collection of the most beautiful light, feel, smell, and sound imaginable. My mother had a soft green incandescence, smelled of oranges and mint and sunshine, felt like *home*, and sounded…well, she sounded like Lily. A painting couldn't encompass the outright *goodness* that was my mother, but my father had certainly tried.

For a moment, I tried to imagine how he must have felt when he lost his one true love for all eternity. Of course she was my mother, and I had beautiful memories and thought about her often, but she was Father's soul mate in the truest sense of the word. I could nearly forgive his anger and bitterness when faced with that realization. Nearly. After all, I was still his son and deserved some of the love and respect that he held for her alone.

Only moments later, I was checking into the Kingston Hotel on the River Lee. *How ironic,* I thought, *that I trade one king for another.* I made my way to the room where my cases already awaited me. As I slid the card into the lock, I heard a pealing laugh and froze.

"If I didn't know better, I'd think you were stalking me."

I turned and almost quivered in excitement when I saw Lily exiting the room across from mine.

"Merely a coincidence," I assured her.

"Well, you better get inside quick or you'll meet the Devil." Her whisper was conspiratorial, but her tone was teasing—perhaps even affectionate.

Already have. Aloud I said, "Are you speaking of Celia? Lovely woman. I relish the chance to meet her again."

Celia appeared behind her daughter and caught the last of my statement. She lifted her head with pride and pushed Lily out of the way.

"Oh, you're too good," Lily muttered.

I flashed a quick grin at her as I took Celia's hand and lifted it to my lips. She must have been forty, but she giggled like a teenager.

"Prince Rioghan, correct?" she simpered. "Or is it Your Highness?"

"Please. Just Rioghan is fine," I assured her.

She tittered, and I had to bite my tongue to keep from laughing aloud.

"Is your father staying here, as well?" She glanced over my shoulder toward my room.

"I'm afraid he's already home." I arranged my expression into one of abject sadness. "He's desperately sorry that he missed the chance to make your acquaintance."

I heard a small snort and swallowed more laughter.

"Well, it's certainly our good fortune that you're still here attending to things, Rioghan. I just realized I never caught your last name."

Lily stood behind her, sticking her finger down her throat and crossing her eyes. I shot her a warning look as my mind whirled.

Technically, I didn't have a last name. Technically, my name wasn't even Rioghan. I'd had many, many names through the ages. Rioghan was given to me a few centuries before, when my father was named Ailbhe, or "world king." Less than a second passed, but I felt myself tumbling into a well of embarrassment as I struggled to think of a last name that sounded regal.

"De Barra," I said, as smoothly as I could manage.

It sounded more like I had blurted it. Lily scowled, but Celia accepted the new knowledge with grace.

"We were about to find something suitable for dinner, Rioghan de Barra. We would be honored if you would join us." Celia glanced up at me through her eyelashes.

Lily was looking at me with hope in her eyes, and it took me off guard.

"The honor would be mine," I said, shooting an inquisitive glance at Lily as I did so.

She smiled gratefully, so I presumed she was glad to have someone along to take the pressure off.

"I'm being totally selfish," Lily whispered as we followed her mother down the hall. "I'll die if I spend another minute alone with her, and I'm not ready to be martyred."

"I'm being selfish, too." I winked.

Her eyes widened quizzically, but I only mocked her expression. I looked behind me and noticed a very large man in a tracksuit following us. With a jolt, I realized that I had already seen him several times, and always when Lily was around. The first time was in Sullivan's when I had met Lily.

"Do you know him?" I hooked my thumb over my shoulder in his direction.

"Who? Dave?" Lily laughed. "He's my bodyguard."

"That's not normal."

"I told you, my life isn't normal."

I contemplated her statement all the way to the restaurant. Lily had chosen a small, private Italian restaurant called Mi Scusi that Celia found unsuitable. Her disdain was written on her face from the moment we stepped inside. Lily did her utmost to ignore her mother, but I knew I needed Celia on my side. It was easy enough without turning on the charm, but I messed with her for the fun of it. I was careful not to cast any spells over Lily. When she fell for me, I determined it would be of her own free will.

"How long do you plan to stay in Ireland?" I asked politely, placing my napkin in my lap.

"There should be someone to do that for you." Celia sniffed imperiously.

Lily rolled her eyes and turned to me.

"Mother is considering a permanent move here. *I* will be leaving in September." Her eyes shone triumphantly as she spoke.

"So soon?" I asked. That didn't leave me a lot of time to play.

"I'll be starting college in the fall."

"My daughter has been accepted to Juilliard," Celia interrupted. There should have been pride in her voice, but it sounded more like envy.

"Juilliard is a very well-respected school." I smiled at Lily encouragingly.

"Mmm, yes." Instead of smiling back, Lily stared at her mother, as if inviting an argument.

"So you've completed the leaving cert, then?" I tried to move the conversation along.

"You mean my high school graduation? In a manner of speaking," Lily gritted out. Getting her to talk was like pulling teeth.

"Lily was under the instruction of several excellent tutors," Celia interjected.

I felt this was supposed to impress me, so I did my best to comply.

"I've certainly suffered my fair share of tutors," I said smoothly. I'd never been to school a day in my life. "I find that, while it's nice to have the one-on-one attention, social skills leave a lot to be desired if one does not attend a school with several of their peers."

Celia nodded thoughtfully and glanced at Lily before murmuring, "Perhaps college can correct this."

"I'm right here," Lily snapped, her expression stony. "Talk about terrible social skills, really."

"Children will get into trouble when left to their own devices, though." Celia continued as if Lily had never spoken. "I shudder at the thought of her drinking or sneaking out with a group of girls to go dancing."

"Oh, please, Mother. This isn't the sixties. We don't sneak out to go the sock hop anymore. We sneak out to cheap motels with our boyfriends."

"That's disgusting, Lily," Celia said calmly.

I chuckled at Lily's grin and knew she had won that battle. And so the rest of dinner went—a humorous battle of wills between two strong females. I was the unofficial referee, first with Lily, and then with Celia, trying to keep them both placated and building their trust in me.

When dessert came, Lily snuck a quick glance at her mother before ordering a coffee. I followed her lead but asked for espresso instead.

"Coffee, Lily? You know how caffeine can ruin the voice. Next you'll be smoking cigarettes." Celia sniffed again.

I thought about handing her a tissue with a wide-eyed, innocent gaze. Lily would get a kick out of it.

"Right." Lily plunked the cup down so hard that the hot liquid sloshed over the side of the cup. "That seems to be the natural progression, doesn't it? Coffee, the gateway drug."

I ducked my head to hide my laughter. To busy myself, I grabbed the bill and settled it with the server. Lily and Celia continued to glare at each other, taking no notice of my generosity.

"Great help you were," Lily grunted when we got back to the hotel.

Celia swept through the lobby, waving off photographers and autograph seekers with a wildly triumphant air.

"What's that supposed to mean?" I wondered. I thought dinner had been fairly pleasant.

"You're supposed to hate my mother. You know, be on my side and all."

"Your mother is truly repugnant," I assured her.

"Wouldn't know it by the way you were kissing up to her," Lily muttered darkly.

"Kissing up to? Do you mean flattering?" I asked.

"Flatter is a rather light term for what you were doing. You were trying to crawl right up into her—"

"Ah, but you'll be thanking me for it later." I winked at her knowingly.

She halted her raving and eyed me speculatively. "What makes you think that?"

"When you want to escape now, all you have to do is say you're going to see me. She loves me. She won't deny you."

"You might be a genius," Lily breathed. She stared for a few seconds more and then threw her arms around me in a jubilant hug. "You're my hero forever and ever and ever, or at least until September when I can escape her for good."

"So thrilled I could be of help," I said dryly. Her arms were still around me, and I began to feel peculiar. It was a nice feeling, being held, and it had been entirely too long. Warmth spread through me, and I moved to place my arms around her waist. She squeezed tightly once more before letting go, and my arms hovered uselessly at my sides.

"I know I sound like this terrible hypocrite, all hot and cold, love her, hate her. I don't hate her. I know she doesn't hate me." She shrugged helplessly. "If that was the truth, I'd have run away a long time ago. But knowing I'm alone is even worse than feeling alone. You don't make me feel alone at all."

Again, her simple, fervent words stirred something inside me. I loved knowing I might be something for her that no one else could.

"Thanks for dinner. I did notice you paid the bill." She turned and entered her suite without another word.

I stared at the door she had shut in my face, and a sense of loneliness crept over me. Melancholy filled my chest, terribly unfamiliar and almost painful. I missed her company, however snarky it was.

I'm going to have to mesmerize her, I thought helplessly.

JENNIFER M. BARRY

λ SE

I woke early the next morning and knocked on Lily's door with bright idea that I might take her to breakfast. I received no answer, however. After standing there a few moments, staring at the door in confusion, I decided to ask the girl at the front desk if she had seen them.

"I'm afraid I can't give that information," she said severely. Her name tag read Vicki.

"Vicki... May I call you Vicki?" I asked. She nodded. The hypnosis was already working. I watched her eyes go fuzzy and then refocus quickly.

"Ms. Murphy is a very dear friend, and I'm afraid that she left something in my possession that I must return to her. I need to know if she has already checked out, or if she might be returning after breakfast."

"Ms. Murphy and her daughter left early this morning for Belfast," Vicki divulged in a breathy voice. She looked faintly dazed by her willingness to break the rules.

"I appreciate your help, and will certainly give your manager a commendation."

"Thank you, sir," she breathed again. She pulled her glasses off and tossed them on the desk as if they had offended her and shook her hair out of the tight bun at the nape of her neck.

Oi. I thought. *Too much, too much.* I turned off the charm immediately, but poor Vicki would be changed for life. At that moment, she needed a cold shower more than anything. She fussed with her blouse, opening the top few buttons and flipping the collar up. I needed to leave before she got completely out of hand.

I made my escape through the revolving door and sat down on the steps. Belfast. The name of the city sent shivers through me. I knew it had become much safer, but during the time of "the troubles" it had been a truly terrifying place. For those that had survived the horror, the stigma would live on forever. I worried for little Lily, praying that she wouldn't step into the wrong pub at the wrong time. I couldn't very well go to Belfast to make sure she stayed safe. She would certainly think me a stalker, then. I had no choice but to wait for her safe return, which would prove Belfast was not the war-ravaged city that it had been just ten short years before.

Unbidden memories rushed into my mind, and I clamped my hands to the sides of my head. Nothing could block out the sounds of the guns that assaulted my brain. In 1972, I had spent several months in Belfast and the surrounding area. It was the worst possible time to have been there, but, as I had been present for every war since the beginning of time, the violence of the IRA felt as if it were on a smaller scale. I had misjudged them.

On a sunny summer day, as I walked from the pub back to my hotel, I had witnessed an act so violent and unexpected that it permanently scarred me. I saw that a scuffle outside the Ulster Bus, but my habit at that time was to walk on by human drama. I was going through an "I'm bored" phase for about the seven thousandth time in my existence. I trudged on, wrapping my wool coat around me more snugly. I had just stepped off the sidewalk when the explosion occurred. My eyes saw the ball of flame that rose from the tiny car, and my skin registered the flecks of concrete, brick, and metal that rained upon hundreds of people in a shower of terror. The silence was unexpected, however. Mouths were open in screams and shrieks. Ambulances arrived on the scene with their lights flashing. Rubble continued to break apart from the ravaged buildings and shatter upon hitting the tarmac. I heard nothing. The whole scene played out like a silent movie, and the loss of that one sense escalated the terror within me.

I had seen the ravages of war, had experienced some of the most terrifying and sadistic things that man or demon could dream. Nothing affected me as much as that scene before me, the senseless loss of innocent life, the abrupt and unexpected attack, the abject despair on the faces of those around me. Everything crowded together in my thoughts and sent a vicious shudder down my spine. I knew, suddenly, that I wanted to help. The edict from my father, the absolute *law* that we stay distanced from others, at once meant nothing. I needed to help those people, not in spite of their humanity but because of it.

Still in slow motion, I moved toward the cause of the commotion. My resolution to give aid flipped a switch in my brain, and suddenly the screams poured over me in waves. Some would live without my healing abilities, and four or five were already moving on to meet their God. One girl reached out with mangled fingers, begging for my assistance. I knelt beside her and saw in her eyes that she didn't have much time. If I wanted to heal her, I had to work quickly.

I put as much reassurance into my expression as I could. She didn't fear me, but I certainly didn't want to give her a reason to start. She whispered something as I knelt beside her. I didn't want to believe what she said, so I blocked it from my mind. Instead, I checked her for life-threatening wounds. From what I could see, she had a large gash on her leg that was bleeding profusely. The entire leg of her jeans was covered in thick, congealing blood, a sign that an artery had been severed. I looked twice to make sure I hadn't missed anything, but that one injury seemed to be the only thing causing the light in her eyes to dim.

I spoke words of comfort, whispering that I would never hurt her and only wanted to help, but she didn't need to hear them. She trusted me implicitly. She whispered the same word again, and I allowed it to roll off my shoulders as I placed a hand over the wound inside her thigh. Concentration was not easy with the melee behind me, but once I felt the heat radiating from my palms, I knew I would succeed.

Only a few moments were needed. As I focused all of my energy on the wound, the blood flow slowed and then stopped completely. The skin began to knit itself together, leaving not even a hint of a scar behind. Color crept back into her cheeks, and her eyes focused on mine. A giddy smile, a side effect of the healing process, creased her face.

"What's your name?" she whispered.

"Rioghan." I gently placed my hand on her forehead.

"Thank you for my life, Rioghan."

Those words would stay with me always. I nearly choked on the tears. "I had no choice."

"Thank you all the same," she said. Then she said that word one more time, and I almost allowed myself to believe it. "You are my angel, Rioghan."

That was the Belfast I had known, a city where twenty-two car bombs had been planted that day. That was where Lily had gone. In my mind, the image of that poor, bloody, war-ravaged girl shifted, and Lily took her place. Irrational fear gripped my heart and twisted. I needed to remain rational, to maintain a level head. She would be fine there. The troubles were all but over. I continued to convince myself as I stood from my position on the steps and dusted my hands off.

With my plans for the morning thwarted, I wandered the streets aimlessly. The sky above seemed to reflect my dismal mood; low hanging clouds were bursting with precipitation. It wouldn't be long before the streets were slick with rain. The branches on the few trees that I passed rattled in the gusting winds, and leaves clung desperately to their perch. Kicking at a beer can that lay outside an empty pub, I thought for a moment about going home to see Father, but shook off that idea.

Things with Ailbhe were very tense, and I avoided uncomfortable situations as often as possible. I could see a movie, but that wasn't much fun when there was no one to share it with. Getting a drink at a pub by myself was sad. I thought about messing around with some humans, but couldn't find the desire. I already had a project, and that was going swimmingly. She hadn't even said goodbye.

I should have some friends, I thought. When had I stopped matriculating with others of my kind? It seemed that everyone I had once considered a friend had somehow disappeared. I couldn't remember when the last had gone. Some had moved to other parts of the Earth for a change of scenery. Some had found love and settled down to family life. The remaining few took exception to my boredom with existence and cut themselves off from me indefinitely.

Three hours were spent in a library, with a book I had read hundreds of times before. I skipped all the boring parts, which turned out to be most of the book. Then I flipped through a few magazines, thinking it necessary to keep up on the trends if I expected to blend with humans on a daily basis. I realized that I didn't care. I only wanted one thing, and that was to see Lily. Even if she was disdainful and attempted to appear callous, I needed to be around her. I wanted to hear that glorious, phenomenal voice again and experience those feelings it awoke inside me. I wanted to feel her in my arms again, even if only for a moment.

"Hiya." The small voice was alarmingly familiar.

"Ciarán." I didn't even turn to see if I was correct.

"Yeah," he replied. I faced him with a sigh and found that he was craning his neck to peer at every corner of the room. "Where's Lily?"

"Not here," I said snappishly.

"I can see that, ya eejit. Where is she?" he said, his eyes sparking.

"I don't make it my business to keep up with her." I stuck my nose into the air.

"She didn't tell you, did she?" He giggled into his little hand.

"Of course I know where she is," I said hotly. "I just don't think it's any of your business."

"Are you in love with her?" he asked. Cheeky little twit.

"No." I sniffed imperiously, and then was struck with how much I must have looked like Celia. I almost flushed with embarrassment, but not quite.

"Oh. You looked like you were lonely and sad. I thought maybe you missed her," he said, winking.

My skin pricked with goose pimples, the kind that appeared after a particularly loving caress. Warmth filled my chest, causing my heart to thud painfully. My stomach clenched and my knees weakened, and if I hadn't been sitting, I would have fallen.

"I'm not in love with her," I said firmly. *Oh, God. I am.*

"Well, I think she likes you," Ciarán said.

My heart swelled again, but I tamped it down quickly.

"Sure she does." I waved my hand dismissively.

"She doesn't act it, I know, but I saw how she looked at you. Like you're a mystery and she wants to solve it. Girls like mysteries."

"How *old* are you?" I cried, prompting the librarian to shush me.

"I'm nine and a half," he said, rolling his eyes. "I told ye I have loads of experience. How old are you?"

"Twenty." I bit the words out impatiently.

He looked me over for a long moment, then shook his head. "You look a lot older than twenty. A lot. You look at least twenty-five."

"You're an annoying little bugger, you know that?" I snapped.

His shoulders dropped, and I immediately felt sorry.

"I get that a lot," he whispered, but then he brightened. "Wanna come play football? We can whistle at the girls together, yeah?"

I started to say no but thought twice. What else did I have to do? So, my only friend was a nine-year-old boy. What a sad existence I had.

"Sure, kid. Let's go."

*

It should have shamed me to admit that I watched every day for a glimpse of her fire-colored hair. I returned to the castle in Cratloe often, but not to think. I watched for her and remembered what it sounded like when the notes of her voice had trilled about the castle's forsaken interior. I was not ashamed and actually reveled in the heart-wrenching, awe-inspiring, appalling, miraculous, disastrous, and wondrous blush of my first love. I could think of nothing else but how her arms felt when she embraced me briefly, the stirring of warmth and joy it had brought to a long-dormant spirit. One moment I was flying high with the memories, the next drowning in despair at the thought of never seeing her again. What if she didn't return to Cork? Would I search every city in every country for the rest of my existence? I realized I would. No matter how Lily aged, I would forever see her as the carefree, sharp-tongued wonder that she was.

I turned to my journal, the only place where I could safely share those thoughts, and poured the agony of first love onto the pages.

It appears I have been struck by Cupid's arrow. If I see him, I'll be certain to kick his ass well and good. The thought of never seeing her again gives me amazing insight into the pain my father must have experienced not once, but twice. I can't believe I was wishing for this only weeks ago. This is too much. I'm quite sure I won't survive this.

A seacht

"You're still here?"

Lily's voice broke into my thoughts. I set down the scone I was trying to eat and smiled, my eyes drinking her in greedily. Her green blouse made her skin look like spilled cream and her eyes like platinum. She tugged the hem of her skirt over her legs and shifted uncomfortably, probably longing for the jeans she usually wore.

Relief at seeing her safe warred with deep affection for the sight of her slender legs, but I couldn't let her see those emotions. I opted for casual, instead.

"I should have asked for butter." I pointed at the offending food with my knife.

"Are you going to live here now?" she pressed.

"I could ask the same of you. When did you get back to Cork?"

"About fifteen minutes ago. Figures that the first person I'd see would be you." Lily crossed her eyes as she snarked good-naturedly.

"What was so pressing in...wherever you went?" I didn't want her to know that I'd been asking around about her.

"We went to Belfast. God, what a gorgeous city," she exulted as she sat down in the seat across from me. "So sad to see the shell and mortar marks in the buildings, even now. I imagine they're left there to remind people of what a turbulent past they've escaped, do you think?"

"Belfast was a terrifying place," I concurred. "I'm glad you returned safely."

"It's perfectly safe now, or so everyone would have you believe. Celia wants to be a part of the peace process, or whatever they're calling it. She honestly believes she can be some symbol of unity or hope. What do you think it is about her that has people so completely fooled?"

"I'm not sure you'd agree with my answer." I smiled to soothe the sting of my words.

"At least try me," she groused, picking at a loose thread on her blouse.

"Your mother is a beautiful woman who knows how to carry herself. She's talented and exudes the image of humility and grace very well. She expects people to love her, and so they do."

"You're right. I hate that answer. You've probably nailed it, though. Why do you see through her, then? You do realize this is the only redeeming quality you have, by the way?"

"What?" I gasped playfully. "You aren't even the slightest bit affected by my dashing good looks?"

"Just answer the question, Romeo."

"I carry with me the wisdom of the ages." I nodded sagely, and Lily elbowed me in the ribs. "That was very grown-up of you."

"I *am* a teenager," she huffed. "I'll act like one if I feel like it. And I feel like it on occasion. Think you might answer the question?"

"Would it suffice if I said I've met entirely too many like her?" I asked after a moment of thought.

"Not really." Lily frowned. "If I met someone else like my mother, I'd probably kick them in their shins on principle. The only reason I don't do that to my mother is that she'd probably cut me out of her will."

"Don't you love her at all?" I asked gently.

"She's disgusting," Lily said, attempting to sound believable, but failing.

I nodded in understanding. In my opinion, her mother truly was disgusting, but I also believed her personality was a product of the life she'd lived for so many years. "But she did give you life."

"Excuse me." She jumped up so that she turned her chair over. "I just remembered that I don't like you."

She stalked out of the café, leaving her seat overturned.

"You'll have to come to terms with it someday," I called after her, talking louder as she moved farther away. "She's your mother. You're her flesh and blood. She doesn't know how, but she loves you too."

And so do I, I wanted to add.

"Nice try, kid." Dave, Lily's bodyguard, appeared out of nowhere.

"Where did you come from?" My heart pounded from surprise.

"If you can see Lily, then I'm never far away." With a shrug, he picked up Lily's discarded chair and sat down. His eyes sparkled with humor and annoyance. "Unless she's managed to give me the slip again."

"Is she always this moody?" I wondered, exasperated.

"You have no idea, mate," Dave laughed. "I've been with her and Ms. Murphy since Lily was eight. She's a good kid, always has been. Completely unaffected by her mum's fame, you know, but she's still scared of turning out the same way."

"Ugh. I hope not." I clapped my hand over my mouth, horrified at what I'd said.

Dave threw his head back and let out a howl of laughter.

"Forgive me. I forgot myself for a moment," I said when I was able to get a word in.

"Ms. Murphy's not so bad, really. She kind of lives in her own little world most of the time, but she's not a mean person."

"Maybe not. But she and Lily…" I let it trail off, not wanting to overstep my bounds again.

"No, you're right. She looks at Lily as more of an assistant than a daughter." An expression of frustration crossed his face as he shared.

"Are you close to her?" I thought his irritation with the situation may have had something to do with his affection for the girl. A smile crossed his face, proving me correct once again.

"As close as she'll let anyone be, I'd wager," he said with a laugh. "She's a prickly one, that girl."

"That's the exact word I use to describe her." I snickered.

Dave's expression turned serious and he leaned in conspiratorially. "I hope you won't give up on her. That little girl needs some friends her own age. I do what I can, but I haven't got a hope of being a true confidant for her. Don't give up, mate. She's still here because she does love her mother, deep down, but also because she doesn't know how to be alone. She's opened up a lot around you."

"R-right," I stuttered. Lily had said as much, but it was good to hear from someone else who loved her.

He was eons closer to her age than I was, but I didn't feel it was prudent to point that out. Dave was a good ally to have, and unintentionally convincing him I was crazy wouldn't have been the brightest move.

Dave offered me his hand, and I shook it slowly, my thoughts whirling. I watched him leave the little hotel café and make his way to the elevators. As I backed my chair away from the table, I wondered how many people had given up on Lily when she needed them and what kind of mother would put her child through such a lonely existence for her own gain.

I vowed to be the best friend I could possibly be to her, no matter how many times she tried to send me away. Prickly Lily was no longer going to intimidate me; she would have to learn to live with my company. Everyone needed at least one friend. I turned the corner, my thoughts still in turmoil, and collided with a solid form.

"Graceful," a haughty voice scolded.

I took a step back to allow the person room to pass, and then realized it was Lily I had almost bowled over.

"Forgive me," I said, smiling. Her frosty expression wiped the grin from my face.

"For what? Knocking me down or that delightful discussion you had with my bodyguard?" she seethed.

"Oh. An eavesdropper, I see. If you were listening closely, you'd know that our conversation was entirely out of concern for you."

Lily's face flushed tomato red, either from anger or embarrassment at being caught. "You... He... I don't need your concern," she spluttered.

"Talk much?" I teased, recalling her scathing words in the castle.

"Ugh." She stalked away, groaning in irritation.

"Are you really leaving this time?" I called after her. "I need to know, see, in case I want to talk about you some more. Can't have you eavesdropping again, now can I?"

"I'm pretty sure I hate you," she called over her shoulder.

"That's too bad, since I love you," I whispered, feeling the weight of those words crush my chest.

JENNIFER M. BARRY

a hocht

July was finally upon us in Ireland. I was still a regular guest of the Kingston and often saw Lily and Celia in the hallways or the lobby. The beautiful weather we experienced didn't soften Lily's attitude, and she ignored me with little effort.

On a particularly warm day, I took book down to the outdoor café at the corner. Warm in Ireland was still cool by most people's standards, but I loved the watery sunshine on my face and hair as I searched for a place to sit. My stomach twisted when I saw Lily at a table in the sunniest part of the courtyard. Dave read a magazine with one eye and watched his charge with the other. She caught my eye, only to look away quickly and grab the newspaper out from under Dave's mug of tea.

The tea tumbled, drenching his lap and a corner of his magazine, and he shouted in protest. For a split second, Lily looked horrified about the mess she had caused, but she lifted the newspaper in front of her face before anyone could see. She knew I approached, and her shoulders tensed with each step I took. Dave swore under his breath as he mopped up the spill, glaring at me when I sat down next to him and chuckled.

"You look bored out of your skull," I commented.

Lily dropped the newspaper she had pretended to read and scowled.

"Dave, aren't you supposed to keep people from approaching me?" she asked casually. "I mean, that *is* your job, right?"

Dave sighed good-naturedly and tossed the crumpled napkin he'd used into the middle of the table. I reached over and picked up the newspaper Lily had discarded.

"Oh, look. A sale on trainers," I said with a smirk.

Lily tried to snatch the paper from my grasp, but I held it easily out of her reach.

"Careful now. We don't want any more accidents, do we?" I teased.

"Dave, seriously. Are you going to do your job, or do I have to do it for you?" Lily persisted.

"Someone's in a grouchy mood, no?" I ribbed good-naturedly as I began to systematically shred the front page of the advertisement insert.

"My mother is doing a concert in Dublin in a couple of weeks. I am, of course, required to go. That was a fun argument, right there." Lily tried to explain.

I wasn't fooled. There was more to it than that, I could see by looking at her.

"That's not all," I prompted. "You're constantly complaining about the concerts, love."

She frowned again at my familiar term.

"That *is* all," she insisted, but Dave chuckled.

"What?" I looked back and forth between Dave's amused expression and Lily's death glare.

"Better go ahead and ask him," Dave encouraged. "You'll have to sooner or later. Celia never takes no for an answer."

"Mind your own business, Dave, or I won't wait until the tea is cold before I dump it on you next time," Lily hissed.

"Ask me what?" I interrupted, growing impatient with the veiled conversation that took place around me.

Lily heaved a huge sigh, rolled her eyes, and growled all at once. It was a pretty impressive sight, as I'd seen plenty of all three expressions, but never at the same time. "Celia has requested the honor of your presence at the concert. She would like for me to bring you as my..."

She searched valiantly for the right term, her face contorting into several different expressions as she considered and discarded several options.

"Date?" I supplied, a thrill running through me at the sound of the word. Judging by Lily's grimace, that was not the term for which she had been searching.

"Oh, gross. Get real," she snapped.

Dave guffawed. "How about arm candy?"

Lily punched him on the shoulder as he threw his head back and laughed even harder.

"I'd be honored to escort you," I said over the cacophony.

How Lily managed to look relieved and irritated at the same time, I had no idea.

"It's black tie. And Celia will, of course, want you to wear something 'royal' or whatever." Her eyes widened in terror as she contemplated the royal dress of Ireland. "Please don't wear a kilt, I'm begging you."

"Got it," I assured her. "Black tie, royal, no skirt."

She grinned weakly at that and propped her chin in her hands. "What country are we going to say you're the prince of?"

I shrugged. "Some random, unheard of kingdom somewhere?" *Oh, I don't know, Tír na nÓg?*

"Guess I'll do some homework. I'd tell her that you're not a prince, and that would get you off my back. It seems, however, that I find your company far preferable to Celia's." She looked surprised by her self-discovery.

"I'll take compliments where I can get them, I suppose." I sniffed, a deliberate impression of her mother, and clutched at my heart, feigning hurt.

"You're not so bad, really. I mean, your feelings about Moira Langley notwithstanding." She offered me a tiny smile.

"I'd say that I was doing this out of the goodness of my heart, but it seems that I enjoy your company as well."

"Aren't you an angel?" she grumbled darkly.

"Not anymore," I teased.

Her brow furrowed as she digested my statement. "You're so weird."

"Ah, Lily, that's not nice. Here I was going to ask you if I could take you to lunch. There's a great kebab place around the corner, but I suppose I'll have to make do with Dave for company."

"What's a kebab?" Lily's brow furrowed in a curious frown.

"Are you for real?" I teased, using one of her favorite American expressions. "Have you been living under a rock?"

I laughed at my own inside joke. Her eyes flashed with irritation, and she stuck her tongue out at me.

"I have not. Just because I don't know what a kebab is doesn't mean I—"

"I thought you'd traveled the world and seen hundreds of cities," I started.

"And eaten in almost that many five-star restaurants," she finished with a pointed look.

"Fair enough. Why don't I show you?"

Dave waved us on, certain that I could protect her without his help. We had just rounded the corner when we heard someone calling for her.

"Lilylilylilylily!"

We both turned on our heels and laughed at the sight of Ciarán pelting toward us on a rickety bicycle.

"Ciarán, love. What are you doing here?" she asked, happiness lighting her face.

He came to a screeching stop and accepted her hug readily.

"It's Saturday." He eyed me suspiciously. "Me brother's home for the weekend, and we're going to play football in the park. I thought you said he wasn't your boyfriend."

"He still isn't," Lily assured him with a grin.

I narrowed my eyes at Ciarán, and the saucy pup stuck his tongue out at me. So much for bonding over football and whistling at girls.

"Where are you going? Can I come, too?" He gazed at her with adoration.

"No," I said shortly. I was rewarded with a punch to the arm from Lily.

"We picked up some food for lunch. Where were you going?"

"Up to Ballyphehane. Would ye like to come?"

"No," I said again.

Lily elbowed me in the ribs. "What park? Maybe we can swing by later in the afternoon."

"The one next to the grotto, across from Lennox." His chubby face was alight with infatuation.

We heard the sound of running feet and looked over our shoulders.

"Oi, kid. Come back with me bike," a tall, ruddy young man called. His face was red from his exertion.

"It's not your bike, ya langer," Ciarán yelled back.

Lily let out a bark of horrified laughter and clapped a hand over her mouth. Ciarán hopped back on to the bicycle in question and began to pedal away.

"See you later?" he called.

"Where are you going?" Lily wondered, running behind him.

"It *is* his bike," he answered, waving gaily as he disappeared around a corner.

Lily collapsed to the sidewalk in giggles. "I shouldn't laugh, but he's such a mess."

"You're a mess," I accused, offering a hand to help her up. She started to stand on shaky legs, still chuckling so hard she could barely breathe. I pulled her up the rest of the way, and she slammed against my chest.

"Oof," she breathed, her laughing silenced.

It was the closest she had been to me since her spontaneous hug almost a month prior, and I wasn't about to let her escape. I wrapped my arm around her waist quickly and held fast.

"What are you doing?" she whispered.

"Making sure you can stand," I lied. She looked up at me then, her grey eyes turning silver.

"Oh," she sighed. Her breath quickened, and I could feel it tickle the hollow at the base of my throat. "You are nice looking. Did you know that?"

"It's never meant as much as it does coming from you." Her fingers reached up and traced the line of my jaw from my ear to my chin.

"That feels nice."

That was an understatement. She was singing without words. Her gaze followed her touch, drinking me in. I knew desire when I saw it, and for that moment in time, Lily *wanted* me. My heart leapt against my ribs, threatening to break through. I pressed my face into her hand, and she trembled, her breath coming in small puffs that warmed my skin.

Suddenly, her eyes changed back to grey, and she pulled away. "I'm sorry. I shouldn't have—"

"It was fine." I assured her. I sighed, wishing I could still feel her there in my arms. "What a beautiful feeling."

"Are you lonely?" she asked suddenly.

"I have been for a while now," I admitted. "Your friendship couldn't have come at a better time."

"But surely you want to be around others like you?" she asked. My heart stopped.

"What do you mean?" I choked.

"Um, nothing, I guess." Her words tripped over themselves. "Forget I said anything, okay?"

What could she possibly have meant by that? What others? Did she know others like me? How did she know what I was? Had Ciarán told her the legends? Did she believe them? I couldn't see Lily as being a believer in fairy tales, but what other explanation could there be? When could she have even seen Ciarán without me there beside her, anyway? Had she seen something that made her suspicious enough to do her own research? I was always careful around her, never trying to mesmerize her or mess about with the weather. Yet she seemed to know it all.

"What are you thinking?" She broke into my thoughts.

I turned to her, carefully keeping my expression blank. Her gaze searched mine, and her face was open and pleasant. She looked like she *wanted* to know my secrets. Ciarán was one perceptive little bugger, I had to give him that.

"That it looks like it might rain," I said, tearing my gaze from hers to look at the sky.

"Ugh. It's always raining here." Rather than the customary frown she wore when lamenting the Irish weather, she smiled. "Let's go get this kebab thing."

Whatever she seemed to know about me, it appeared she had accepted it readily enough.

A naoi

I walked briskly, enjoying the weak sunlight. More so, I enjoyed the thought of whom I was going to see. We were in Dublin, a fair city. Life was beautiful, the River Liffey was beautiful, and for the first time in a long time, I felt as if there might be some purpose to my existence. My journal entry for the morning certainly reflected my joie de vivre as clearly as any mirror possibly could.

For the first time, I'm considering sharing my secrets with someone. I know that didn't end up working out for Father in the past, but I'm sure this is different. I truly believe Lily is one of a kind and created for me. Perhaps that is the most self-centered thing I've ever thought, which is saying a lot, considering my less than humble attitude of late.

All I know is that when I'm with her, I feel free. I feel like centuries worth of worry are lifted from my shoulders and I can breathe. If I had known love could feel like this, I might have attempted it sooner.

Because I had my own home in Dublin, I had no excuse to stay in the same hotel with Lily and her mother. That did not stop me from waking at an obscene hour, ready to make the trek to the Regency Hotel. I was afraid Lily would not be up and about yet, but as I turned the corner and made my way through the crowded streets to her hotel, I stopped short and laughed. Lily, my beautiful Lily, sat on an upturned milk crate, talking to the filthiest tinker I had ever seen. I would never cease to be amazed at her complete lack of self.

"Well, Rioghan, imagine that. Here you are in front of my hotel. Again." Her smile was kind, but her words were biting.

"Lily, my love," I said by way of greeting. My eyes flicked to her companion, and he grinned. I tried not to laugh when I saw that he had but three teeth.

"Frankie, this is my friend Rioghan. Rioghan, say hello to Frankie. He lives here." She said it with such finesse, as if she were graciously inviting me into Frankie's well-appointed home.

"Hiya, Frankie," I said. If Lily could treat the situation as normal, then I damn well could, too.

"Good to know you, Rioghan," Frankie replied, offering a knotty, grizzled hand.

I shook without hesitation and turned over another milk crate to join them.

"Frankie and I were people watching," Lily explained with a huge grin. "Let him amaze you with his insight."

I raised my eyebrows and turned my gaze to Frankie who shrugged.

"Been watching people for a while now," he offered by way of explanation.

"Here, Frankie, what about this guy?" Lily interrupted.

I followed her gaze to a thirty-something man who wore a cheap suit, black loafers, and a watch with a shiny steel band. He gazed at said watch and ran his fingers through his over-long hair.

"Oh, he's a sad case, he is," Frankie decided.

I stared at him, impressed. I believed he was right, but needed to know what made him so sure. "What gives you that idea?"

"Well, he has a white indent on the ring finger of his left hand. That marriage ended a month ago, if I'm right. His shoes are good, but his suit is cheap, so she's got the money. That watch must've been a gift from the missus, the way he's gazing at it. Like he might see her face there if he looks hard enough. Wonder if he cheated and is regretting it, or if she's the cheater and has left him heartbroken."

"Quite impressive," I allowed with a nod.

Lily's eyes were bright with enthusiasm. "What about Rioghan? What can you tell about him?"

"Rioghan's too easy," Frankie said with a sniff.

I was offended...and curious.

"Well now you have to tell me." I laughed, but inside I was cringing.

"Right, so." Frankie shrugged. "You're rich, but you don't like it, except that it means you get to do whatever you want to do whenever you want to do it. You'd rather be normal most of the time. History bores you, because you feel that's all you have. And you think you've finally got some hope for the future. Is that about right?"

"How could you know?" I gasped.

He was so spot-on that it was eerie.

"Easy. You're wearing jeans and runners. Normal. But they're good jeans and runners, so they cost a lot of money. Your shirt is worn, but it was probably over a hundred euro brand new. There's a look about you that says you're not pleased with your past. And I sense a lot of hope, which makes me think that the future is where your desires lay."

"You missed some things, but I have to say I'm pretty impressed," I said with a laugh.

He had a curious way of speaking, with old-world charm mixed with uneducated slang. Frankie was a conundrum.

"I didn't miss nothing. I left some out because nobody wants their secrets aired," Frankie said, his brown eyes searching mine.

For a moment, I believed he did know every last thing about me. It was downright spooky, but it made me like him more. Perhaps it was because, if he did know my secrets, he was willing to keep them that—secret.

"Don't be all offended, Rioghan. He described me the exact same way," Lily teased, punching me lightly on the shoulder. "Only he knew that the past was important to me, because the future scares the bejesus out of me."

"Yes, you're a good match, you are," Frankie said wisely. "You'll help each other through those difficult areas and become stronger people in the end."

"We're not a match," Lily objected, turning over her milk crate in her haste to stand.

"No?" Frankie eyed her appraisingly.

"No way. Rioghan doesn't even like girls."

"What?" I yelped. That was news to me.

Frankie tossed his head back and roared with laughter. "Oh, he likes the ladies all right. You in particular. Can't you see he's dead gone for you?"

Frankie seemed delighted in his new role as matchmaker. I wanted to shut him up somehow, but I could only stare balefully at Lily as her emotions worked over her face.

"You're not?" she whispered, backing away from me.

I shook my head slowly.

"I'm many things, but I'm not gay," I said, reaching for her. She took another step back and stumbled over her makeshift seat. I stooped to help her stand, but she wriggled out of my grasp.

"Why do I feel like you lied?" she whispered. Her lips were white and trembling.

"I can't tell you, love." My voice was as calm as I could manage. "This changes nothing, Lily. Please don't back away from me. I still cherish your friendship very much."

"He does," Frankie interjected solemnly.

I shot him an annoyed glance, silently begging him to butt out.

"You *are* a stalker," she shrieked. "I knew it. You're always everywhere I am, and you're always trying to do nice things. And the way you suck up to my mother. It's disgusting."

"Lily, no." I reached for her again, but she jerked her arm from my grasp and ran up the steps to the hotel.

I stood, frozen to the spot, and watched her go. She turned once to look back, concern etching her features, but it was for Frankie, not me.

"She'll come around," Frankie said. "She loves you, too."

"It's not much comfort right now," I moaned.

JENNIFER M. BARRY

A Deich

"What are you doing here?" Lily asked snidely.

I was unable to answer, having had my breath stolen when she opened the door. Her copper curls were gathered in a shining crown on top of her head, threatening to break loose and run wild. A flush of anger colored her usually creamy face, and the roses that bloomed on her cheeks were so lovely I wanted to brush them with my fingertips.

"You look stunning." There were no other words to describe her.

"You didn't answer my question," she snapped.

"I promised to escort you to your mother's concert this evening. I don't like to break promises."

"You're uninvited." The frost in her voice made me smile involuntarily.

"It would be a damn shame to waste this suit. I'm afraid I'll have to go, anyway. Oh, and imagine your mother's reaction when you show up without me."

She glared at me silently, and I knew I had won the argument.

"You look stunning." I tried again.

"Thank you." She forced the words through tight lips. "You look very nice, too. But I'm sure you were aware of that."

I was very aware, but it meant so much more when she said it. The suit hugged my shoulders like a lover, as it had been made to do. The tailoring perfectly emphasized my stature, making me appear taller, broader, and wealthier than any man had a right to be.

She sniffed disdainfully, and I chuckled out loud. Prickly Lily was simply too delightful.

Her hand twitched at her side, and then she gave in to her urge to touch. She started at my shoulder, pretending to brush away invisible lint. Dragging her fingers down the sleeve of my jacket, which was made from the finest wool, she nearly brought me to my knees. Crisp white cuffs peeked from the sleeves, and she lightly traced the cufflinks she found there. I'd had them made especially for the event. If she'd looked closely, she'd have seen the faint impression of lilies in the metal, but she reached instead for my silver necktie.

As she gripped the fabric under the pretense of straightening it, I said, "I've asked your bodyguard if I might have the honor of escorting you without a chaperone."

She glared for a moment, pulling me toward her menacingly, but then her expression cleared.

"I don't have to ride with my mother?" she asked.

"Nope," I replied, using one of her American terms.

Her lips were right there, inches from mine and pursed so beautifully. My pulse quickened as I imagined what they'd feel like against my own. She would resist for a moment, but then she would have to give in to the warmth and the want, the love and the...

"You're forgiven." She let go of my tie and gently pushed me backward.

"Well, that was easy enough." I laughed, shaking my head to clear it. "I'd like to apologize for the misunderstanding. I'm not sure what led you to believe—"

"Forget it." Lily waved her hand, looking more like her mother than she would ever want to believe. Her flush was back, but it was embarrassment rather than desire. "Assumptions."

"Ah, because I also would like to be normal? And my father and I have different 'lifestyles?'" I queried.

She bit her lip and nodded shyly.

"I can see where that might cause some confusion."

"So what does make you different, then?" she pressed playfully. "Can we play Twenty Questions?"

"We don't have time for twenty," I warned, taking her clutch and tucking it into my jacket.

"Okay, then. Animal, vegetable, or mineral?" she teased.

"I'm afraid that even if I answered that question truthfully, there would still be too much to explain."

"You can't say something like that and then drop it."

Her eyes were bright with curiosity, and I contemplated sitting her down to describe my existence.

"No, that would take too long," I muttered.

She sighed and clenched her teeth in aggravation.

"Perhaps I could show you?" I mused.

Her eyes lit up and she nodded enthusiastically.

"Fine, then. If you'll come along now, so as not to irritate your mother, I'll show you what I mean."

"Tonight?" she pressed.

"Absolutely. If we are to continue to be friends, if I am to continue to fall in love with you, it's only fair that you should know the whole truth about me."

"You are the prince of some crazy, unheard of country, aren't you?"

"Lily, let's go," I said huffily.

Why did she completely ignore my declaration of love? The thought brought a sharp pain, but I was determined not to get discouraged. If she could act completely unaffected, then so could I.

She sat down on the bed, arranging her silver gown so as not to wrinkle it. I stood by the door, watching her struggle with her strappy shoes and considered offering to help. Knowing the right move was hard. On one hand, she could appreciate the assistance; on the other, she could resent my intrusion.

"A serial killer, maybe?" she tried again, looking up from the intricate buckle.

I snorted.

"A *spy*? Oh, oh. Are you in the Irish Mafia? Am I on your hit list? Or better yet, my mother?"

"Perhaps you watch too much television. You should take an umbrella. It will be raining soon."

"Fabulous," she muttered.

I extended my hand to help her stand, and she accepted readily. As we approached the elevator, I smiled at our reflection in the decorative mirror. I had brushed my long hair back and secured it with some pomade. My tie matched her silver dress. I hadn't been aware she would wear that color; I had chosen it because of her eyes.

"We look like we're going to the prom," she grumbled. "But you do look handsome."

I caught her eye in the mirror and winked. "Thank you. I imagine that little compliment was very hard for you."

When the elevators opened in the lobby, we groaned in unison. The rain I had promised was pelting down at an alarming rate. The wind alone would surely destroy our vestments for the evening, even as we tried to find a taxi. Because of the weather, there were no taxis to be had. Lily growled deep in her throat, opened the umbrella with a snap, and took off at a fast pace in the direction of the theater.

"We aren't going to make it."

She ignored me, as she was wont to do, and continued to march down the street, sidestepping the tiny rivers as much as possible. Her shoes were totally unsuitable, but I knew that to say so would be taking my life into my own hands.

"Slow down, love, or you'll break your ankle," I warned as a gust of wind turned her umbrella inside out.

"Is it always raining in this freakin' country?" Lily shrieked, tossing the useless accessory aside like garbage. "And stop calling me 'love.' I am not your love. It's your fault we missed riding with Mother and Dave. And for the love of Godiva, why did I pick these stupid shoes? Oh, that's right. I *didn't*. My mother did, as well as this ridiculous dress that's sticking to me like Saran Wrap in this rain."

Her dress had indeed begun to cling to every inch of her petite form. My fingers itched to trace the lines of her hips, caress the planes of her back. The rush of desire that filled me was shocking. I'd imagined kissing her, holding her, pressing close to her, but never so much as I did at that moment in the pouring rain. What had been a hope turned quickly into need. I wanted to grab her, fold her into my arms, and help ward away the shivers that were wracking her small body. While I tried to keep these new emotions under control, she worked her way up to an atomic outburst. I panicked and dragged her into an empty alleyway.

"What are you doing? Are you molesting me?" She fought my every step, but I was much stronger. "Hey. Hannibal Lecter. What are you—"

I swung her around, and her harangue stopped abruptly.

"That's right. Please stop freaking out on me."

I was pleased with the response my normal words received. She simply stared, but her eyes still darted back and forth with panic.

"Now, I'm going to do something that will make you want to scream again, but please don't. I'm only doing this to help you. Please trust me."

The wind began to slow and the pelting rain turned to mist. I kept my gaze on hers, willing her to stay silent. It would be hard enough without her imminent reaction. An eternity passed, and I watched the wonder in her eyes as the clouds began to part above us. We were still sheltered in the shadow of the narrow alley, but the sunlight sparkled cheerfully on the wet pavement inches from our toes.

"Are you doing this?" she whispered as I conjured a warm breeze that caressed her cheeks and hair.

I nodded, my gaze burning into hers, hoping against hope that she would remain calm. She lifted her face to the wind and smiled the first real smile I had seen on her face.

"It's beautiful. Please don't stop."

My father would be furious. When he became aware of the change in the weather pattern over Ireland, he would have no doubt his own son broke that particular rule. Her delight was worth the wrath I'd suffer.

Her curls, once matted to her head, dried in casual disarray. The air had released them from the clip that never seemed to hold them anyway. She looked down at her dress to find it waving gently in the breeze, as dry as it had been when she donned it in the hotel room. I breathed a sigh of relief, certain I could hold my newfound desire at bay as long as she was decent again.

"What are you?" she murmured, raising her chin to stare at me once more.

"Better you don't ask these things yet." I tapped her nose affectionately. "Are you ready now? We might make it now that we're not fighting the wind."

I offered her my arm and she took it cautiously. As we darted down the sidewalk, I chanced a quick look at her face. The wonder slowly slipped away, and absolute panic once again took its place. I struggled to think of something to take her mind off what had just transpired.

There was no need, it turned out. At that exact moment, a tiny dark-haired girl crashed into us. We both sighed as the bags the girl carried split and dumped her new clothes all over the sidewalk. The girl stared desolately at all of her purchases, then raised her eyes apologetically. When she saw Lily in her silver goddess dress and me in my tuxedo, she gasped and lifted her hand to her throat.

"I'm so sorry," she whispered. Her eyes were a muddy brown and filled with tears.

"What are you sorry for? We weren't watching where we were going either. I'm afraid I was distracted." Lily shot a dirty look at me, as if to say that it was all my fault.

I shrugged, accepting the blame readily. Lily was already on her knees, having dragged her dress up so it wouldn't get soiled. The mousy little girl and I both watched in awe as Lily gathered up the contents of the bags. She was quite a sight—the pale folds of her dress billowing in the breeze that I continued to conjure, the delicate shoes somehow kicked off and set aside, the dazzling array of titian curls—on the ground, selflessly offering her time. I snapped to attention and bent to help, but the petite brunette still watched with her mouth hanging open.

"I don't know what we'll do about your bags," Lily said, tipping her face to the stranger. "They're destroyed. You can't carry all this without new ones."

She laughed lightly as she held up a paper bag that had ripped down two seams, shaking her head in defeat.

"I'll go get more," I offered.

"No, I—" the girl started, but I was already gone.

I glanced at my watch and considered calling Lily's bodyguard, Dave, to let him know we were running late. He had a history of covering for her. I nodded to myself, the decision made, and dialed the number as I pushed through the doors of the closest shop.

"Hi, Dave, it's Rioghan," I said by way of introduction.

"Where are you?" he hissed. "Is she okay? Has she been hurt? Her mother has gone mental."

I chuckled at the image, picturing Celia with her hair pulled out and lipstick smeared. It was a lovely vision, but I knew that wouldn't be the case. She probably stood stock-still somewhere, her face white with rage, assuming some embarrassment had been thrust upon her.

"We're fine," I assured him quickly. "I appreciate that you allowed me to escort her by myself, and I apologize for the delay. I'm afraid we had a run-in with someone and caused her to drop her purchases. We're on the other side of the park now, but you know Lily. She lifted her dress and sat right down to help the girl pick everything up. I'm getting some new bags to replace the ripped ones now, so we'll be on our way soon."

Dave heaved a great breath, and I knew he was silently cursing Lily's enormous soft spot.

"You left her alone?" he asked, almost as an afterthought.

"Relax, big guy. I can see her from here. She's laughing with the girl that almost ran over her. She'll be in good spirits when we arrive," I assured.

"Well, that's something, I guess. I'll do my best to keep Celia occupied, but please hurry."

"Tell her I'm bringing a gift from my father," I suggested. "Tell her he had to remove it from a bank safe-deposit box and this is why we're running late."

"You're a genius, kid," Dave said heartily. "I don't know what you'll do about finding a gift, but that's your problem now."

"I can handle Celia." I smiled confidently.

"Right. You're the only one," he uttered, hanging up.

I turned my attention to the shopkeeper and was out the door with three large bags in moments.

"Thank you so much, Rioghan," Lily said.

I handed her the bags with a smile and noticed that she and the girl had folded the spilled clothing neatly in preparation.

"This is Aisling," Lily continued as she loaded up the merchandise.

I smiled brightly at the girl, causing her to blush and stare at the stone walk.

"We're going to meet her for coffees as soon as we can get away from the concert. Oh. The concert. We're so late. Mother will wonder where I am."

"No worries. Dave promised her a gift from my father." I winked.

Lily relaxed and rolled her eyes. I handed Aisling the bags, and we promised to call the second we escaped Celia.

"So what are you going to give my mother that might possibly make her forget that I embarrassed her again?" Lily asked. There was a dark tinge to her question, but her face was still alight with excitement at the prospect of a new friend.

"This," I said, pulling a box from my pocket. I had intended it to be a present for Lily, but it had become abundantly clear that keeping her mother happy would be the better gift.

"Oh," she said, surprise rendering her incapable of further speech.

I opened the slim case so that she could see, and she gasped. "How could you know she'd love this? This is seriously perfect."

I was observant; that's how I knew. The satin lining cushioned a brilliant platinum choker with an emerald the size of a fifty-cent piece.

"Is it real?" she asked, looking up at me with unspoken accusations.

I snapped the box closed and stuck my nose in the air. "Of course it's real."

"Did you steal it?" she tried again.

Utterly affronted, I stared at her with all the ire I could muster. "Absolutely not. This ornament has been in my family for centuries."

Lily groaned. "And you're going to waste it on Celia."

"There's more where this came from," I said stiffly.

We had barely touched on my superhuman status. I didn't dare tell her when or how those baubles had been created, nor by whom. I almost chuckled at the thought of her reaction if I told her the leprechauns had crafted that priceless necklace.

"Green is her favorite color," Lily mused. "Well, it has been since she decided that Ireland is her forgotten home. Really, I think she decided that Ireland has a better economy than America at the moment, and therefore has more money to spend on her."

"What's your favorite color?" My query seemed mundane enough.

Her face went blank for a moment while her brain processed the normality of the question.

"Um, red." She nodded decisively.

"And why red?" I asked, expecting her to spout passion, love, anger—anything but what she said.

"Celia says it's vulgar." Her face was smug.

"You like red because your mother hates it?" I asked, very sad that she didn't seem to have her own opinion on the matter.

She shrugged as if her reason was perfectly acceptable.

"And your favorite movie?" I pressed, wondering if I wanted to know the answers anymore.

She didn't even think about it before answering. *"Mommie Dearest."*

"Do you have any feelings or emotions that aren't the opposite of what you're expected to have?" My heart broke for the girl who had never been permitted to develop her own personality—a girl trying to hide her own heartbreak because the love she so desperately wanted had been denied.

"I love singing," she muttered. "And I hate that I love singing."

St. Stephen's Green was in sight, the last bit of our walk before we reached the theater where her mother would give an evening concert.

"My whole life has been dictated, from what clothes I wear to what subjects I study in school," she shared. "The future has been planned for me since the moment I was conceived. Celia wanted a little girl, and I complied, even then. She hated my red hair, and not only because, in her mind, red is vulgar, but because it reminded her of her childhood here. I guess I don't have to tell you that things were awful in the sixties and seventies."

I shook my head with a small smile, but wasn't allowed to say anything because she jumped right back in without pausing for a breath.

"She says her parents were unbearably poor. I think she spent the majority of her childhood praying that she had been adopted and her real parents were royalty somewhere. I'm sure she dreamed they'd come to rescue her someday, which is ironic because I've always wished some normal family somewhere would come and take me away."

As she spoke, I became lost in the memory of the absolute poverty her mother claimed to have lived through. Ireland was a land of much suffering and had been for over a thousand years. During the decades that Lily had mentioned, times had been especially rough. I remembered strolling through Dublin and seeing children in cloth diapers that were filthy beyond words. The housing tenements where they lived were constantly spray-painted with the phrases and nicknames of gang members. Teenagers were sent out to steal food for the family, however they might. Water was added to soup, various roots to coffee, and bread was a precious commodity. It would certainly be a hellish childhood for anyone to survive, even for Celia, the devil-woman.

"I don't doubt life here was hell on Earth. I've seen movies and read books about it, but even those probably don't... It was like a third-world country in some places. She didn't exactly steal, at least that's what she says, but she did save up every penny she found to pay for the community drama program," Lily said. "At first, it was probably the cheapest and safest way to stay out of the house, but I think she eventually enjoyed losing herself in other characters, you know? When she was sixteen, she was discovered by an American film producer and, like an idiot, she married him and escaped to his castle in Los Angeles. In his defense, he did make her famous, and then she dropped him like a greased football and married her next victim—my father. That marriage was even shorter than the first, and it wasn't her last.

"I think they divorced when I was a year old, and I've only seen him twice in my whole life. She's tried to mold me into a mini-Celia, and it turns out that's exactly what I am. I can't live without singing…or her, it seems." Her voice broke off, and she brushed away a tear that threatened to spill over.

"Anyway, I was trying to explain why she hated my red hair. She dyed it blonde for the first time when I was only five. I had scabs on my head from the chemicals, but she would sit behind me and brush out the curls until I looked like her. She had these stupid dresses made for me that matched the ridiculous gowns she wore on stage."

"You're much better than your mother," I started, thinking it might comfort her.

"Oh, I've never heard that before," Lily told me cynically.

"Of course you've heard it before," I snapped, growing impatient with her. We had strolled halfway around St. Stephen's Green before I was able to speak, and then the words I spoke only served to push her further away. "Your voice is the most incredible instrument I've ever heard. And I've heard angels sing."

Lily glared at me, but there was a hint of incredulity to her expression. "I hate it when you say things like that. You're freaking me out."

I dismissed her with a wave of my hand. "Oh, you hate everything I say."

She gave a half-smile at the veracity of my statement.

"Why does it bother you so much that I'm so taken with your voice?"

"Because everyone is," she huffed. "I say this not because I'm proud but because it's true. 'Oh, Celia may I take your coat? Oh, Celia aren't you lovely? Oh, Celia may' I please kiss your—'"

"I wasn't complimenting your mother," I interrupted with a wry grin. "We were discussing you."

"Yes, well, most people seem to think that it's the same thing." Her eyes were sad, and I wanted to comfort her somehow.

What is this feeling? Why this girl? Is it merely her voice, or is it because she seems completely oblivious to my charms? She had warmed up, but there was still a wall there, solid and unyielding.

"What do you mean by that?" If I kept her talking, I would find some chink in that armor.

She closed her eyes and sighed, coming to a standstill in the middle of the walkway.

"Like I said, my mother is the most famous opera singer the world. I've been to lots of countries, seen a bunch of cities and opera houses, met heads of state and other celebrities, and I've never wanted for a thing. Well, not many things." Her voice was strained with the effort of speaking the words. "I've had people at my beck and call, fawning over me, lusting after me, sending me flowers and love notes. It's ridiculous. I can't have a normal conversation with anyone. I've never had a slumber party, never experienced a real first date. All they want is the notoriety that I can give them.

"And then, as if things couldn't get any worse, it turns out I can sing, too. And the general consensus is that I'll be better than my mother. God, I can't tell you how that made things Hell on Earth for me. My mother, who only saw me as an accessory, a shiny bauble, doesn't want me around. Of course, you wouldn't know by the way she treats me in public. I'm her little doll, her brilliant, talented trophy."

"So you hate the gift," I whispered.

She nodded, tears welling in her eyes. "I don't want to hate it. I love to sing, love it more than anything in the world. I don't want people to hear it. I don't want people fawning over me the way they do my mother. I want to know who I am and not who others think I am. I want…"

"What do you want?" My voice was more intense than I had intended, and she looked up at me.

"I want to know that someone loves me for me."

Just like that, I was lost. The world became a spinning vortex, losing all constraints of time and space. What was past was gone away, wiped clean, and I was born again. She had stated it so simply and with such fervor that I had no choice but to comply.

"I will," I murmured.

She froze, her eyes wide, and I hoped that she would trust me. Prayed, pleaded, swore, and bargained with the powers that be that she knew I meant it with all my heart.

Her eyes narrowed, and the breath was stolen from my body. She didn't believe me.

"Don't be stupid."

The park exit was within sight, and she quickened her steps to avoid walking with me. I sighed and let her walk ahead, knowing that she would wait for me at the theatre door. She didn't dare face her mother without Prince Rioghan. I wondered why Celia had never bothered to ask me what country I might be the prince of. It probably didn't matter to her, so long as I was royalty and interested in her daughter. Royalty trumped opera singer any day.

She waited right by the doors where I thought she'd be. I watched her trying to tame her curls, using the reflection in the glass. She caught my eye and dropped her gaze to the ground. Her fingers were still tangled in her hair, worrying at the clip, but she wanted to give up and leave it wild.

"It looks lovely down," I offered.

With a sigh, she dropped her arms and shot me a crooked grin.

"It looks like a bonfire," she countered with a snicker.

My heart soared with relief as I realized she was no longer angry with me for overstepping my bounds.

"I think it looks more like spun gold."

I reached out cautiously to remove the clip. The curls sprang forth, covering her shoulders and slinking down her back against the silver dress. She looked like a statue made of precious metals, frozen in place from my touch.

"I'm sorry I ran," she whispered. "I appreciate your friendship more than you could ever know, but I keep pushing you away for some reason."

I cupped her cheek in my hand, and she leaned into my touch as if she craved it. "You have trouble trusting, and I understand that. Until I met you, I wasn't someone *anyone* could trust, but I promise that you can trust me now, even if I don't expect you to."

Stroked her cheek gently with my thumb, I watched her intently for a response. Her eyes were silver again, and I was beginning to wonder if that happened often, or only when I was touching her. She was very still, but I felt her tremble under my fingers.

"Are you cold, love?" I asked, beginning to shrug out of my jacket.

"What? No." Her eyes widened, and I wondered what was going through her mind. "I mean, yes. It's cool out here. We should go in before my mother sends Dave to find us."

The pre-show cocktail party came to an end, and Celia stood by the stage door with a strained look on her face. She nodded tersely to anyone who dared to approach her and wish her luck. She saw me before Lily, and panic crossed her face. I brought Lily around in front of me and smiled as Celia's face crumpled with relief. Before Lily could say hello, that look was replaced with anger.

"Lily." Celia's voice was cold.

"I'm sorry, Mother," she said meekly.

"Your hair looks ridiculous," Celia sniffed.

"Yes, she tried to tell me that, but I still wouldn't let her put it up," I said smoothly. "I think it looks beautiful, but she says she looks like a—what did you say, Lily? A bonfire."

Celia allowed a small smile and nodded in agreement. "You missed the entire party. I do hope you'll grace us with your presence at the after-party?"

"Again, that is my fault. My father wanted me to bring you a token for luck. I tried to tell him that wishing a performer good luck is actually bad luck, but I'm afraid he didn't understand."

Delight crossed Celia's face at the mention of my father. I pulled the slender box from my pocket and opened it, presenting the choker with a regal air. Her hands flew to her throat, and she gasped.

"Isn't that beautiful," she breathed.

I removed the necklace from the satin lining and opened the clasp. "May I?"

She turned excitedly and stooped so I could place the jewels around her slender neck.

"It's perfect," I told her when she turned to get our approval.

"It does look lovely, Mother," Lily said, taking Celia's hand. Her mother gazed at their clasped fingers, and I thought I saw tenderness in her eyes.

"I will see you immediately after the performance." Celia's eyes went hard again.

Lily let out a long breath and dropped her arms to her sides. "Of course, Mother. Rioghan and I will be waiting right here for you."

"Well, that could have been a hell of a lot worse," Lily said as her mother disappeared from sight.

"Should we find our seats?" I offered, extending my arm.

"Are you always such a gentleman?" She placed her hand in the crook of my elbow with a sigh.

"Is that not preferable?" I asked, fully confused.

She looked up at me, her silver eyes twinkling softly, and a small smile touched her lips.

"It makes it hard to hate you." Her voice was barely a whisper.

"Well, in that case, a gentleman I shall always be," I chuckled.

"I was afraid of that."

"It *is* okay to like me, Lily-girl," I teased. "It doesn't mean that you must trust me."

"They kind of go hand in hand for me," she insisted.

We found our places at the front of the theater, and I helped her into her seat. Much to my amusement, she fussed with her dress, smoothing it this way and that, before giving up and balling the extraneous fabric into a lump in her lap.

"She's going to kill me when she sees that I wrinkled a perfectly good Galliano gown," Lily groaned. I sat down next to her and continued to watch out of the corner of my eye as she smoothed the material over her lap again.

"It's no use," she hissed, flinging her hands into the air. "I'll look so rumpled for the photos."

"Absolutely not," I assured her. "We'll take care of it, love."

"With your magic?" She peered at me through her lashes.

She looked so open and excited about the mysteries of my world, however practical she'd always been in the past. Her silver eyes sparkled, her breath hitching as she waited for my answer. In fact, she looked like she awaited a kiss rather than mere words, and the thought sent a thrill of desire straight through me.

"Something like that," I finally responded.

Love was excruciating, really. I didn't know what I could do or say to let her know how I felt about her, or if she would ever return the feelings. She was warming up to me, learning to trust me. Did that mean she might someday feel the all-encompassing love I felt for her? Did she already love me and refuse to acknowledge it?

I remembered how her body had trembled when my arms were around her that day in front of St. Finbar's Cathedral and how she had looked at me as though I was her entire world when I conjured the breezes to warm her in the alleyway. There surely something there. Was I going crazy, finally, with the whole of eternity stretching out behind and before me?

a haon deag

She fit into my arms as if she had been formed to be there. Our gazes locked as we began to move, feeling the music as if it were a shared heartbeat. I felt the party guests watching, all of them wondering who we were, but admiring us all the same. Lily's delicate hand squeezed mine in solidarity, and I pulled her even closer into my embrace. It was the most intimate feeling, having her there, breathing the same breaths. Gliding effortlessly across the dance floor, we were locked together in our own fantasy world, where my father and her mother didn't exist and bodyguards weren't waiting around the corner with watchful eyes—a world where her imminent death and my perpetual life had no bearing.

She allowed me to lead, which was unexpected. Lily struck me as the kind of girl who did the leading at all times, so her tiny offering, her gift of control, meant more to me than any words she could have spoken.

"You have so many secrets in your eyes," Lily remarked as we started the second dance.

"Do I?" I asked, startled by her statement.

"Oh, you know you do." Her lips curled upward slyly. "You hold them to you like your treasure."

"As I'm holding you now?" I queried.

She didn't blush or drop her gaze but stared even more intently.

"What are you?" Her voice was a whisper, but I could hear it clearly over the din of the party, clanging plates, tinkling glasses, and surging orchestra.

"Let me preface by saying that I will have no proof to back up my statements," I warned. "What I tell you is the absolute truth, but you won't believe a word of it."

Lily looked frightened at that point, so I tipped her face up gently.

"Go on," she whispered. "I've seen you do some incredible things, so I'm ready for whatever you tell me."

"I'm a fairy, Lily. Old as the Earth itself, and yet only as young."

She froze, her silver eyes wide with the disbelief I had prayed would not appear. "Say that again?"

"A fairy. I'll be happy to tell you the whole story, if you like?"

"Like six-inch-tall, wings, and pixie-dust fairy? Tinkerbell?" She shook in anger, pushing against my chest to escape my embrace.

"Tinkerbell?" I scoffed. "You wound me."

"Are you messing with me? Really? Fairies aren't real." Her voice grew louder, and I looked around cautiously to ensure we weren't overheard. "I'd have had a better chance of believing you *were* a serial killer. Or a spy. Or a demon. Hell, you could have sworn you were an angel and I would have believed you. You give me *fairy*?"

"I swore to myself that I would never do this to you," I whispered. She trembled with rage, her face white and her fingernails digging into my arms. "I'm going back on my promise to myself, but only to calm you, right, love? Only to calm you."

As I spoke the words, I covered her with waves of peace and tranquility, hating myself the whole time for manipulating her. She deserved her own thoughts and feelings, even if they led her in the opposite direction. Despite my confliction, her body relaxed, as I had known it would. Her grip slackened and her eyes became unfocused.

"Now, love. I'm going to leave you so you can process what I've told you. You won't speak of it until you're ready, right?"

She nodded.

I hated myself for charming her.

"You'll do whatever research you need to do to believe me, but you will believe me. When you think you want to hear the rest of my story, you can seek me out and I'll be more than happy to share."

I walked her slowly to an empty table, filled a glass with red wine, and helped her to sit. She accepted the glass and drank deeply.

"Oh," she muttered, her eyes focusing again. "What is this?"

"I believe it's a cabernet," I said lightly. It amused me to no end that she could find fault with the wine when she had so many other things on her mind.

"A pinot noir might have been nicer," she commented. "Sorry, that sounded like something my mother would say. I should have just said thank you. I don't even know the difference, to be honest."

I chuckled and plopped down in the chair next to her. I had told her I was leaving, but she was too irresistible. Lily played with the stem of her wine glass for a few moments, and I gave her the time she needed to gather her thoughts.

"So you're not a demon, then?" she finally asked.

"What makes you think I'm a demon?" I was insulted and amused at the same time. It was amazing how close she could get to the right answers and yet be so very wrong.

"You're so smooth and slick, like," she said, a Cork accent coming through the longer she sipped her wine. "It's what I've always imagined a demon would be like, if I were to meet one."

"Oh, they're slick, all right," I assured her. "You'd be struck dumb by their beauty, were you ever to meet one."

"But *you're* beautiful," Lily started, and then stopped herself. A blush bloomed across her neck, and I was sure that she said more than she had meant to.

"As are you, my love." My words embarrassed her further, but the roses on her cheeks were too lovely.

"Why me?" she whispered. "How would you, the most mind-numbingly gorgeous man I've ever met, find anything to love about me?"

"I'm afraid I pursued you because you didn't seem to think I was handsome." Heat suffused my cheeks as I admitted that.

"Of course I did," she snapped, making me laugh.

"And there's the second reason. Your waspish temper keeps me on my toes. I'll admit that I've had women falling at my feet for centuries, but you, love, were the first to ever make me doubt my own allure. It baffled me, so I tried harder. The more I learned about you, the more you drew me in. You're humble to the point of self-deprecation. You'll sit down on the ground in a dress designed by a master to help a stranger pick up her packages. Little boys and homeless men are welcomed into your huge heart easily, and yet you've kept me at arm's length. You're an enigma, wrapped up in a mystery, with a big secret on top. I've fallen hopelessly in love with you, my Lily."

She leaned toward me, as if to tell me a secret. Our faces were only inches apart when she spoke.

"People say that they love me all the time." Her expression and voice were mournful. "No one's ever meant it. Not even my own mother."

"You already have too much to process right now," I acknowledged, brushing my thumb over her cheek. "You may forget that I have declared myself, if you wish."

"That's the best part," she whispered, tears forming. "Don't take it back. Not you, too. Please." Her words were tremulous. "Please love me."

For the second time in my existence, my world rocked at its very foundation. Perfect, unchanging Rioghan had been transformed. "Of course I won't take it back, my love. You may be assured of my devotion to you, whatever else you decide to believe."

A DO DEAG

It had been three long days since I had declared myself to Lily. After the party, we met with Aisling for coffee as Lily had promised, and then I went on back to Cork while Lily and Aisling had a three-day slumber party. I wasn't sure what a slumber party entailed, but I sincerely hoped there had been gossip about me.

I had to wait one more night to see her. The next day, I planned to drive back to Dublin and return her to Cork City. Because Lily wanted to prolong her freedom as much as possible, we were going to stay overnight somewhere along the way. She'd already asked Aisling to join us in Cork, so I was looked forward to a car full of girls for at least two days. At one point in my existence, that might have made me cringe.

As I kicked a pebble down the sidewalk, feeling lonely and sorry for myself, a familiar voice called for me.

"Ciarán?" I asked, narrowing my eyes to see the form approaching from across the bridge.

He was on his stolen bicycle again, so I deduced the owner hadn't caught him.

"Where's Lily?" He came to a screeching stop in front of me.

"You know, it hurts my feelings that you're always asking for Lily. Aren't you ever glad to see me?" I pasted a mock scowl on my face.

"No," Ciarán stated plainly. "You're not nearly as good-looking, and you're a *boy*. You're all right to play football with but useless if I want to hold hands."

"You won't be holding her hand any time soon." I laughed, shoving away the brief prick of jealousy at the thought. He was only a boy.

"You're her boyfriend now, then, are you?" His shoulders slumped.

"You'd probably have to ask her that," I replied.

"Well, I knew it was gonna happen, like," he said gloomily. "I could see that ye liked each other. Think she'll still be my friend anyway?"

"You'll not get rid of her that easily," I assured him, clapping a hand on his shoulder.

"Ah, sure, there's more fish in the sea, right?" His posture straightened, and his tummy poked out over his jeans.

"I'm going to see her tomorrow." I wasn't sure what possessed me, but the next words were, "Would you like to come along to Dublin with me?"

"Do you mean it?" Ciarán's face lit up. For a moment, I was stunned by his brilliance. In his single flash of joy, Ciarán was beautiful to me.

"We'd have to check with your mother, of course," I said, when I was able to speak again.

"Ah, she won't care."

"We're planning to stay the night in Wicklow. I won't let you come if I don't talk to your mother and make sure it's okay."

"Ah, fine," he grumbled. "Got a phone?"

"We'll find one," I said resolutely.

"How do you not have a mobile?" Ciarán's eyes were incredulous.

I bit back a chuckle, thinking that I already laughed at him too much. I was sure to hurt his feelings.

"I've never once needed one before this moment," I told him honestly.

"No friends?" He was sympathetic as he laid his little hand on my arm. My throat closed for a moment as I shook my head.

"None to speak of." My honest answer seemed to shock him almost as much as it did me.

"Well, you should get a phone. I'd call you. And I bet Lily would like to call you, too."

"You're not so bad, kid." I cuffed him on the head before hooking my elbow around his neck. He shrieked playfully as I dragged him with me down the sidewalk.

*

"Hiya," Ciarán said as Aisling situated herself beside him in the backseat.

"Hi," she said, her voice quiet but her smile bright.

"You're beautiful, you know that?" Ciarán continued.

"Now why does that sound familiar?"

Lily teased him, but Ciarán didn't even have the decency to blush.

She climbed in after Aisling and settled herself in the passenger seat. Her eyes sought mine and held for a long moment, so I tried to tell her with my gaze how much I had missed her, how beautiful she was to me, how I'd give anything to hold her.

"Lily makes me wear cosmetics now."

Aisling grumbled, but I could see she found rouge and mascara worthwhile, if her pleased expression was anything to go by.

"And you look lovely," Lily trilled from her spot in the passenger seat.

"Thanks for inviting me along today," Aisling said shyly. "I was facing a day of doing dishes and talking to my dog."

"What's 'is name?" Ciarán wanted to know.

"Adonis," Aisling shared, her cheeks coloring with shame.

"What kind of name is that?" Ciarán blustered. "Why does everyone I meet have stupid names?"

"He must be a handsome dog." I chuckled as I steered the little car through the streets of Dublin expertly.

"If I had a stupid name, I'd change it," Ciarán announced to no one in particular.

"What would you change it to?" Aisling wanted to know.

"I wouldn't change the name I have. It's not stupid. Ciarán's a cool name. I just mean if I *did* have a stupid name. Why didn't you name your dog something cool, like Buster? Or if you were going with the whole mythology thing, you could have called him Titan or Hercules, right? Wimpy Adonis."

"Little mythology scholar." Lily's eyes flashing mischievously. "How do you know about Adonis?"

"Yeah, I like to read. Told you that already," Ciarán muttered.

"Well, it does surprise me, since the last time I saw you, you were riding into the sunset on a stolen bicycle. When do you find time to pick up a book in between all your thievery?"

"You didn't," Aisling gasped.

Ciarán stuck his chest out proudly. "I did. It's a good bike, too."

"You should give it back, you know," Aisling suggested.

Ciarán snorted and punched her in the arm. "Who are you? Mother Theresa?"

"Not even close." Aisling shook her head at the impossible boy beside her.

"So how come you don't have a job?" Ciarán asked bluntly.

"Oh, ah. I do. I'm a teacher." Aisling's cheeks filled with color.

"Yeah? What d'ye teach? Not grammar, I hope. I don't want you correcting me the whole trip."

Aisling tittered nervously and shook her head. "No. I teach, um, sciences?"

The word came out like a question, but I was the only one who raised an eyebrow.

"Well, good. If you can handle a whole classroom of eejits, you can handle me," Ciarán stated.

"I'm sure I'll figure something out," Aisling assured him.

The rest of the ride was spent admiring the Irish coast. We drove south from Dublin through Dun Laoghaire, where we got out of the car to have a quick lunch. Aisling had packed a bag of cold chicken, pasta salad, and bottled water. We ate on the concrete steps that led to the water and watched the waves crash over the rocks, reveling in the cloudless sky. After we polished off the last of the chocolate chip cookies the girls had made during their sleepover, we climbed back into the car and headed into the Wicklow Mountains.

Low, wispy clouds began to converge. They ringed the hills, obscuring the peaks and lending a mystical quality to the landscape. The sun was not deterred by the clouds and painted the wildflowers along the hillsides as we drove. The late July air was crisp and warm as it rushed through the open windows. Lily had put in a CD of rock music, and she and Ciarán sang together in harmony. Aisling's eyes were closed, and her face tipped toward the sun. A small smile danced across her lips every time Ciarán sang a line that was incongruent with his age.

A strange feeling filled my chest as I observed them all. I couldn't remember having people like them in my life before. I'd had friends, but none that gave me such a sensation of being complete.

Lily reached over and took my left hand in hers. I couldn't take my eyes from the road, but that one little act of acceptance annihilated me. It was the first sign she had given me that our conversation at the concert gala really happened. When I left her in Dublin, it was primarily so she could sort through her feelings and have a good chat with another girl. I hadn't been sure what to expect from the trip, but I had hoped for a welcome reception. I would not pressure her in any way.

My eyes locked on our entwined fingers, and I was staggered with the implications. She wasn't the type of person to take any sign of physical affection lightly, and that made her touch even more profound. What had once been a small gesture to me was, in fact, the largest thing in my world at that moment. I was accepted. My love for her was welcome.

As we drove on toward the Rosslare Peninsula, Johnstown Castle loomed before us. I heard Lily's gasp of incredulity.

"Can we go inside at all?" Ciarán queried, struggling free of his safety belt. His face appeared between the front seats, and his eyes were wide with wonder.

I wanted to break the rules for him. It wouldn't have been the first time I'd done the opposite of what I should have. Lily contemplated the outcome of breaking and entering and finally shook her head.

"I think probably not," I warned, following her lead.

"That's no fun." He pouted, turning his devastating lower lip on the girl of my dreams in the hopes of convincing her.

"I'd be no role model for you if I allowed that, now would I?" Lily laughed, impervious to his charms.

"Besides, I assured your mother over the phone that we'd keep you out of trouble." I felt like a father with my stern tone.

"Ah, me mam's used to trouble. I kicked the windows out of the convent last year, and she only shook her head at me. Didn't hit me or anything."

"Ciarán," Aisling gasped.

She was fighting back gales of laughter, and she wasn't the only one.

"Sure I did. They're only nuns, aren't they?" Ciarán challenged.

Aisling could no longer control her laughter. It burst forth in silvery waves, stunning all of us into silence. It was one of the most beautiful sounds I had ever heard.

When she could speak again, Lily said, "You should laugh more often. Just the sound of it makes me happy."

Aisling clapped her hand over her mouth and blushed furiously. Ciarán grinned at her, poking his tongue through a space where a tooth was supposed to be but had yet to grow in. Silvery giggles erupted again, washing indescribable emotions over all of us.

"Your laugh is even prettier than you are," Ciarán stated.

Aisling chuckled even harder. "Aren't you the little flirt?"

We took another picnic lunch to the Italian Garden. Lily and Aisling spread a quilt for us and then passed around cold cut sandwiches and crisps. Ciarán bypassed the sandwiches and went straight for the oatmeal cookies the girls had kept from us.

It was only half six in the evening, but the sun began to fade. The few clouds that had gathered were a brilliant pink and cast a glorious reflection in the man-made lakes that surrounded the castle. We disposed of our rubbish in a bin before beginning our exploration of the grounds.

Ciarán was sullen when I reached for Lily's hand. Before I could feel any sympathy for him, he grinned and blinded me once more with his beautiful joy. Then, without another word, he grabbed Aisling's hand and dragged her down the path. Lily and I heard them both shrieking in laughter as they ran.

"It's magical here." Lily spoke in hushed tones, pulling her blue cardigan around her tightly. We had stopped along the path to gaze at an older castle ruin that bordered the lake, and the breeze from the water was chilly. "I can almost imagine the Lady of the Lake offering up Excalibur to King Arthur."

"It wasn't in this exact spot, but the setting is eerily similar," I said without thinking.

She froze, her fingers turning to ice in my hand. "It *is* a myth, right?"

"Some parts," I acknowledged. "Time and word of mouth have built absurd versions of the truth."

"There was a King Arthur?" Her voice trembled.

I wondered what was running through her mind. I wanted nothing less than to frighten her. She was obviously more curious than scared, so I saw no harm in expounding.

"Very certainly, there was."

"And an Avalon?" she pressed.

"In a manner of speaking."

It wasn't a very satisfying answer, but there was so much more that needed to be explained before we touched on the mythical Avalon.

"And Merlin?" She expected a negative response to her question, but it was not something I could give her.

"Merlin does exist."

She caught the verb tense and the corners of her lips twitched in amusement.

"As does Morrigan, or I guess you might know her as Morgan le Fay. And Mordred, Arthur's son with Morgause. They all exist. Well, all except Mordred. He was killed shortly after Arthur was taken to Tir—I mean, to Avalon."

"I want to say that it's all impossible," she said, walking slowly down the path again. "I've seen so many amazing things since meeting you, though. There's too much to process, you know? Is Merlin a nice guy?"

"Emmm. I suppose he is, if you don't get on his bad side."

"So he's a fairy, then?"

"A sprite, actually." I snickered at the look of consternation on her face when I corrected her.

"I'm still digesting fairy. Don't throw sprite at me, now," she chided.

"I'm sorry, love. I forgot myself."

Lily walked in silence, her lips pressed together in thought. Her fingers trailed gently over the blooms that lined the walkway. I knew she wanted to ask. I waited patiently and was rewarded when she took a deep breath to begin her questions again.

"Just for the sake of superfluous knowledge, what exactly is a sprite?"

"An ancient spirit that has been trapped here on Earth," I said matter-of-factly.

"A ghost?" Her eyes narrowed in disbelief.

"Very much more powerful than your everyday ghost, I should think. He's been around almost as long as I have and has learned many, many secrets of the universe."

"So where does he live, then?" Lily demanded.

"Everywhere, and nowhere."

"Cryptic answer," she accused.

I had to laugh. "I have a hard time imagining that Merlin has a home. It's been centuries since I've seen him, and at that time he had taken up residence with my father."

"What does your father have to do with all of this?" Lily's eyes were as round as saucers.

"Too much, love. There's too much to explain, and I fear you'll never even know the half of it."

She stared at me for a few moments, apparently wondering if she should press the issue. Finally, she shrugged and nodded. "You're probably right. I feel my head might explode if you tell me that one more crazy story is actually real."

"I could blow your mind."

JENNIFER M. BARRY

A TRI DEAG

The Cliffs of Moher were an astounding sight, even to someone who had seen them as many times as I had. The sheer rock face climbed from the violent ocean, and the mist of the crashing water carried several hundred feet to kiss the faces of those who dared to venture close enough. The vast green of Ireland rushed right to the brink of forever, plummeting over the side without a care in the world.

At one point, visitors could step out to the very edge of the precipice and stare down into the waves, but the need for safety dictated that a wall be built and the most dangerous areas of the park be closed to foot traffic. We thumbed our noses at the *NO ADMITTANCE* signs and crossed the lush grass to the brink. It was foolish to subject Lily to such danger, but there was no comparison to facing down the pummeling winds of the Atlantic. The West of Ireland was constantly under attack by rain and gusts, making a stroll along the edge of the world a risky venture, but Lily met the danger head on with a trilling laugh that told me she enjoyed the peril.

"Please be careful," I cautioned her.

She waved off my concern and flopped onto her stomach. Creeping inch by inch, as a snake in the grass, she cautiously peered over the steep precipice. I lay down next to her and propped my chin on my hands.

"Wow." Her eyes were closed, and droplets of seawater clung to her lashes, looking like tiny diamonds. "It feels like I'm on the very edge of the world here. When I close my eyes, I can imagine the Earth drops off into nothingness, into deep blue sky and stars."

"It makes me feel rather insignificant," I admitted. "It's humbling to see something so brutal and battering as the waves there."

"You mean your fairy-ness wouldn't be any kind of match for a little bit of seawater?" Lily teased. She rolled onto her side and studied me from the corner of her eye.

"It's not so much that, really," I said. "Sometimes I remember there are things more eternal than I am. They're not easy to find, but when I do, I'm staggered by them."

Like this love I have for you, I thought suddenly.

"Why didn't Aisling come along?" I asked, trying to change the subject. I wasn't sure how open I could be with my emotions.

"She says she hates heights." Lily giggled. "I can't imagine her missing this on purpose. She and Ciarán have been hanging out non-stop since she came to Cork, anyway. I shudder to think what kind of trouble they're getting into today."

"You mean, what kind of trouble Ciarán's getting her into," I corrected with a grin.

"She seems happy enough staying in the hotel. She loves Mother—God knows why—and lets Mother pick out clothes for her. I think it's been good for her self-esteem. I wonder who her friends were before we came along?"

"I dare say she didn't have many," I mused. "She seemed a very withdrawn soul."

We sat without speaking, listening to the roar of the sea below us.

"So, you think you'll ever tell me what it is you are?" Lily asked suddenly.

"Are you sure you're ready to hear these stories?" I studied Lily hopefully. "Can you handle more?"

"I've been to the library, scoured the Internet, bought book after book on mythology, and nothing answers my questions. I've been searching for answers for weeks now, and I haven't found anything about how you could change the weather and whatever else you can do. I look at you and think that maybe I already know, deep down, what you are and where you came from." She trailed off, her eyes bright.

"Is this the whole demon from Hell thing again?" I growled the words.

She flashed a sheepish grin, but shook her head. "Not so much Hell."

I shifted uncomfortably. She'd nearly hit on the truth without my help, even if she didn't know it.

"All right, then. I'll start at the beginning. It's been several millennia," I started.

Lily shuddered. Whatever she said, and no matter how much she thought she meant it, she still wasn't ready to accept the story of my origin.

"Do you want to hear it or not?" Irritation crept into my voice.

Lily rolled over onto her back and pulled me closer. Since she had done her own research, she found it easier to accept the truth from a book than my lips, but something had changed. She wanted to know my side, my experiences.

"Several millennia..." she prompted.

I marveled at the way her eyes turned to molten silver in reaction. Seeing the love that I felt for her, love I had waited thousands of years to experience, reflected in her eyes had the power to bring me to my knees.

"Have you heard 'In the beginning'?" I started again.

She smiled and nodded, pulling my head onto her shoulder and twining her fingers through my hair. It was such a delicious feeling that I wasn't sure I could continue.

"Well," I said after a moment, "this is absolutely the truth. Heaven and Earth had only the angels to inhabit them. You probably have heard the story of the fallen one, Lucifer? Also true. When Lucifer made his move on the Kingdom, he was cast out forever, and the gates of Heaven were sealed."

"And you were around for this?" Lily asked in a hushed tone.

"Not exactly." I could see her confusion. "There were thousands of us roaming Earth that day, the day God shut the doors forever. My father and I were away, merely out having fun, and never even knew what happened. Lucifer had his followers, but we weren't a part of them. That didn't matter to the Father. When we made our petition at the gates to re-enter, we were denied, grouped in with those who had revolted, and we've walked the Earth since."

Lily studied my face for several moments, struggling to accept my story as fact. Her fingers traced the lines of my face, and I could see that I had finally reached her.

"You're an angel?"

"No, love. When I was barred from Heaven, I was an angel no more. Neither am I demon, as I chose not to join Lucifer and his minions. I'm merely a fairy, and will continue to be for all eternity."

"Merely," Lily snorted. "There's nothing 'merely' about being a fairy, even if you've had thousands of years to get used to the idea."

"So now you know. And now I want to know more about you," I said, sitting up.

"Nothing I could tell you would interest you." She turned her head away, staring sightlessly at the line of cliffs.

"On the contrary. I've never been more curious. Some of the deeper workings of your mind are already apparent to me. I don't, however, have any idea where you were born."

"Los Angeles," she said promptly.

"Really? Your mother's second husband was from LA?" I asked, raising my eyebrows.

"Yup. We lived there until I was a year old. They divorced, and she and I moved to New York. She married a guy there, too. He didn't like me much. Actually, I don't think he liked her much, either."

"And you've lived there ever since?" I prodded.

"We moved to London when I was eight. That's when Dave joined our merry little band."

"I quite like Dave," I mused.

"Me, too. I don't remember who I talked to before him. I didn't need a bodyguard then, but Mother had a scare with a stalker around that time, so..." Her voice trailed off, and she shrugged.

"Sounds like she was worried about you."

"If she was, then that's the first and last time she worried about my well-being." Lily sighed in resignation. She dug her fingers through the grass at her side and pulled up a few strands. "Dave's been cool, though, and he's saved me a few times from crazy stalker people. There was this guy in Philadelphia that said God told him I would be his wife. I mean, what the...? I was only fourteen, for cripes' sake."

"Does it still scare you? Knowing that people know who you are and where you're going to be?" I struggled to keep my voice soft, but my concern for her safety tried to fight through in a scream.

"I won't lie. Sometimes it scares the bejesus out of me. This isn't something you get used to, you know?"

"I'm certainly starting to see that. When do you get to have fun?"

"When I'm with you," she said simply.

My heart skipped a beat, and before I could stop myself, I placed a kiss on the top of her head.

"I guess I've had fun before. Some of my tutors were a blast. My music teacher did a lot of stuff on the Beatles, Pink Floyd, Elvis. She was cool, and my history tutor was always taking me to historic sites in whatever town my mother had dragged us to. I mean, for a girl my age, I've seen a lot of stuff. I can't complain about that. My science teacher taught me how to make fake blood, and I used it to give Dave a heart attack." A guilty smile crossed her lips as she relived the memory.

Because she was much more open and honest about what was in her head, I ventured a question, hoping for a more honest answer.

"Is your favorite color still red?"

She looked at me for a long moment before shaking her head. "I like it, yes. But I think I've decided that I'm more partial to blue."

"A decision that has nothing to do with your mother," I crowed triumphantly. "I'm so proud of you."

"And my favorite movie is *Breakfast At Tiffany's*," she added, after a moment of thought. "I used to take a cab and stand in front of the windows, like Audrey Hepburn did in the movie. I love how she refuses to grow up, kind of lives a made-up fantasy life until she's forced to look life in the face."

"Keep talking," I encouraged. I was thrilled to watch her blossom before me as she divulged each little secret. Her careful façade slipped away, and she eagerly showed her true colors.

"I love Moira Langley. Oh, hush. I know how you feel about her. And Evelyn Todd. Giulio Maroni was like my uncle when I was growing up, well, more like a great-uncle. I cried oceans when he died."

Her effusive praise for her favorite opera singers warmed my heart. It was wonderful to hear her embracing her gift, even if for a few moments. I couldn't comment, because she continued on in a rush. Once the floodgates were opened, there was no stopping her.

"My favorite food is salmon, but not smoked salmon because that's slimy. I hate green beans with a passion. Um, I kind of hate being so short because I've always looked younger than I am. And I'm scared senseless to go to Juilliard in September."

She stopped short after her last confession and stared at me in surprise. Apparently, she hadn't meant to share so much. Her eyes began to shine with tears, and she blinked furiously to keep them from spilling onto her cheeks. I reached for her hand and pulled her into my lap.

"Why are you afraid?" I whispered. "You have no reason to doubt yourself. You're a brilliant singer, and you'll blow them all away."

"Thank you. I'm not scared of that. Singing is my refuge, no matter how good or bad I might be. What terrifies me beyond all belief is I don't know if anyone will like me." She rushed the last few words and then buried her head in my chest.

"Shh," I comforted, running my fingers through her soft curls. "Of course they will, my love. You're kind and funny. You're lovely and talented. What's not to like?"

"I don't know how to be around people. You should know more than anyone. I was horrible to you, and it was only because I was afraid I'd end up liking you and you'd disappear on me."

"I'm not going anywhere, sweetheart."

"Has it occurred to you that *I'm* not always going to be here?" Her voice was tremulous as she spoke.

My heart gave that peculiar twist as I pondered her words. Was she talking about leaving for college? That would have no bearing on our relationship. I'd go with her. I'd go anywhere with her, for the rest of her life. Oh. Life. Which meant death for her someday. That would be a problem.

"I'll be with you until you draw your last breath," I vowed.

JENNIFER M. BARRY

A ceachair óeag

"I'll never forget that moment when I heard you sing," I murmured, burying my nose in her hair.

She shivered and scooted closer on our perch.

"Were you sitting right here?" She gazed around the castle ruins, where we had stopped impulsively on our trip back to Cork from the ring of Kerry.

"I was. The Earth stood still, and everything I had been searching for finally found *me*. I remember thinking that the birds and that little brook over there must be jealous beyond belief that this mortal could create magic more potent than theirs. You know, I loved you in that moment."

"But how could you? You didn't know me."

"But I did. When you sing, your mask is dropped and you are suddenly free of all your pretenses. I heard all the pain and sadness you carry with you, enough to kill a weaker mortal. And yet, there was also joy and hope. So much love, seeking a resting place, a home. I wanted to be that home for you."

Lily thought a moment before she responded. "And you are home, amazingly enough. I don't know when it happened, but you've become the most important person in my life in just a couple of months. I didn't even know how much I needed you."

"You don't have to sound so astonished, love." I feigned hurt, rubbing my chest over my heart.

"Oh, did I hurt his little feelings?" She plunged her fingers into the hair at the nape of my neck as she mocked me.

I bit back my reply as I relished her touch.

"Thank you for not giving up on me," she whispered, her hand beginning to still.

"Would you understand if I told you I couldn't?" I murmured in response.

"I think maybe I would." Her gaze sought mine. Once again, her eyes were a mysterious silver, and I lost myself in their depths.

This should be game-over time, I told myself fiercely.

There wasn't a single girl in my long history who'd been around longer than the morning after. Loving and leaving was what I did best, but Lily was different. Just the thought of leaving twisted my heart into an unrecognizable form.

"Your eyes are incredible. Did you know that?" My words were barely audible, but she shook her head.

"They're nothing like yours," she breathed. "I've never seen anything like them. It must be the years of joy and heartbreak over things that I'll never know, never comprehend—so much wisdom and mischief, misery and triumph. How could I possibly compare?"

"You don't." She looked taken aback by my statement, but I grasped her hand before she could back away. "You outshine all."

She simply stared, her mouth parted in awe. I studied those lips, which had spoken words that could rip a man to shreds, and knew there was nothing more beautiful. Even agape, they curved into a tiny smile. I couldn't stop my forward motion as I placed a tiny kiss on the upturned corner of her mouth. When she didn't pull away, I gave attention to the other corner. Her breath quickened, and her fingers tightened at the nape of my neck before she stilled.

Gently, ever so gently, I placed my lips on hers. She sighed, and my brain turned to mush. I couldn't have prepared for my reaction; my vision went white, and stars seemed to explode outside my range of sight. Her mouth was soft and sweet, shy and inexperienced, but it set me on fire and erased every kiss I'd ever given or received before.

I allowed her to lead, scared I might overwhelm her with the intensity of the unchecked desire coursing through me. I was soaring, tumbling, careening wildly through the air at the innocent press of lip against lip, and then grounded when her slender arms tightened and pulled me closer. If I had to spend eternity on Earth, I wanted to do it while kissing my girl.

"Mm, wow," Lily breathed as she pulled away. "Is this what it's always like?"

"What?" I asked, my brow furrowing.

"You know. Kissing." Her cheeks flamed, and she ducked her head in mortification.

"Never before," I said honestly. The meaning of her words sunk in. "Wait. Do you mean you've never been kissed?"

"I know; pathetic, right?" She pulled her hair around her face to hide her shame.

My beautiful, talented, heartbreaking girl with the voice of an angel had never before been kissed. Was every man blind?

"Not possible," I finally uttered. My head still reeled, both from the intensity of our shared kiss and the implication that I was the very first, ever, to share such a moment with her.

"Well, it's true," she said, mistaking my astonishment for doubt. "You don't have to believe me."

"I do, my love, I do. I'm overwhelmed that you would choose me." An unfamiliar emotion swept through me—humility. Lily had humbled me. "I'm honored. Amazed and honored."

"Yeah," Lily said, her face flushing even deeper. "Wow, that was eloquent."

I didn't want her to stop thinking about kissing me, but I also didn't want to make her uncomfortable. Only thing came close to the miracle of her mouth. My heart straining with hope, I asked, "Would you sing for me?"

"Of course. What would you like to hear?" She kicked her legs over the wall so that she faced the interior of the castle.

"You choose first, and then I'll teach you one," I offered.

"All right. I'll sing *Un Bel Di* from *Madama Butterfly*."

Without any further comment, she opened her mouth and turned my world upside down once more. Oh, the emotion and melancholy that she could elicit with a few notes. I leaned my head against the cool, stone wall and watched as she wandered around the ruined tower room, giving attention to the medieval stronghold with little touches and caresses. Her eyes focused somewhere in the distance as she became totally unaware of her surroundings.

After the last note finished ringing, she dropped her shoulders and stared at the floor. With a small movement, she kicked a loose pebble across the room.

"I get so lost."

"As do I," I assured her.

"It's so easy to get caught up in another person's life and struggle and forget my own. I guess in that way, I understand my mother more than I care to admit."

"You aren't like her. Not at all."

"She wasn't always this bad. I guess I'm afraid that if she could change so drastically, I could, too."

She ducked her head and studied her shoes as if she were afraid to see any agreement in my eyes.

"But you understand the danger. She didn't know what she was up against with fame and money. Don't for a second think you can't overcome the temptations that kind of life can throw at you. You're stronger, smarter, and more courageous than that."

Before I could even get the last word out, Lily had flown across the room and into my arms. Breathlessly, she peppered my cheeks with kisses, murmuring thanks in between each one. I put up my arms playfully, as if to ward her off.

"You're very welcome, love. Now, let's sing some more?"

I helped her to the floor, onto the quilt that she had brought, and she laid her head in my lap. The sun began to set, and brightly colored clouds peeked through the gaps where a solid wall had once stood.

"O, a wan cloud was drawn o'er the dim weeping dawn," I murmured, my voice barely causing a stir in the air.

"Mm," Lily sighed. "Your voice is beautiful, too."

She snuggled closer with her eyes closed and a dreamy smile on her face. I stroked the line of her brow as I continued to sing *The Foggy Dew*, and after a few moments, she began to hum along. Her voice created intricate harmonies with my baritone, though she didn't know the words.

"Would you come with me to meet my father?" I asked.

It was an impulsive request. I hadn't even thought through the implications or the potential outcomes, and once the possibilities began to crawl through my head, I wanted to retract the invitation. Lily's eyes shone with excitement and trepidation, however, and I couldn't bring myself to speak the words that would make that disappear.

"Scary." She shivered a bit but smiled. "Will he like me, do you think?"

I didn't know how to honestly answer that question. I placed my palm against her cheek and caressed her as I formed my answer.

"My father doesn't like humans as a rule," I started.

She nodded, almost as if she had been expecting that answer.

"He was hurt by one very badly, I'm afraid, and has never been the same since."

"It's not fair that he should judge me by someone else's actions," Lily murmured. "But I suppose I've been doing that most of my life, haven't I?"

"How do you mean?" I pushed an errant curl from her forehead.

"Shutting people out my whole life because I feel like Mommy didn't love me. Just because she's not great at showing affection doesn't mean everyone is like her, right?"

"I hope not." I laughed and pressed a kiss to her forehead.

"You make my heart skip a beat when you do that," Lily whispered.

"What? This?" I teased, kissing her temple gently.

"Yes." The word came out in a breathless hiss. Her heartbeat raced as my lips traced a line down her jaw.

I covered her mouth with mine again, chastely but with purpose. Her answering moan awoke the desire I'd been holding at bay. Without thinking, I swiped the tip of my tongue over her bottom lip, begging for entrance from the girl who'd never been kissed.

As I should have expected, she stiffened immediately and clenched her teeth. Her welcoming sighs turned to whimpers of distress, and I pulled away to reassure her.

"Sorry, love. I got carried away. We can stop."

"No, I liked it," she insisted. Her cheeks flushed, and she covered her face with her hands. "I'm just so..." She was lost for words, and all the different Lilys flash across her face as her mind attempted to right itself. "I've never done this before. I want to, but I really don't know what I'm doing or how to make you feel good."

With my fingers at the nape of her neck and thumbs under her chin, I angled her face so she could see my smile. "My heart nearly exploded when I kissed your cheek. You make me feel good just being, I swear. Kiss me, Lily."

Her head tilted back, her body melted, and she invited me in. With slow, deliberate strokes, I teased her with my tongue, growing bolder as she opened to me and returned the kiss with ardor.

I crushed her against me, dragging my fingers up the length of her spine. Her skin was silk to my touch, warm and smooth, as I tugged the hem of her shirt up to feel more. I wanted her. I'd wanted her from the first moment she turned her nose up at me, but that first stirring of longing was nothing compared to the way my chest clenched with each shuddering breath. I held myself in check, fighting the searing heat of desire urging me forward. She wasn't ready for more, and if I didn't stop then, I wouldn't be able to.

"We should go," I said, releasing her.

"What?" Her eyes were unfocused, and her lips—oh, God, her lips—were swollen and pink and the most beautiful thing I'd ever seen.

I gave her a moment to collect herself, trying to pretend I wasn't deeply affected as well.

"I don't want to," I assured her when embarrassment tinted her cheeks. I never wanted her to think she was undesirable. "Trust me, Lily. I *really* don't want to stop, and that's the problem."

"Fine." Obviously hurt again, when that was the last thing I wanted, Lily at least allowed me to help her to her feet.

She followed me to the crumbling staircase and clung to my shirt as we descended. When we reached the waist-high grass at the foot of the castle, she spoke again.

"So who hurt your father so badly that he hates all humans? Was it a girl? Did he fall in love with a girl?"

"He did," I answered grimly.

"Oh." She looked surprised that she had guessed so easily. "Anyone I might know?"

I glanced over to see if she might be open to the truth. She danced gracefully around the fallen stones, twirling the quilt behind her like a flag. I grinned as I watched her joyful steps. I hoped I could take most of the credit for that unabashed happiness.

"Well?" She stopped mid-skip and turned to me.

"Oh. You may have heard of her, yes."

She frowned, and I knew she was running through the names of historical figures in her head. "She was a queen or something, wasn't she? Mary, Queen of Scots? Queen Elizabeth?"

"She was a queen, yes. She was a queen because she married a king. I believe she was a mere mortal before she met my father and made him love her."

"Like me?" Lily asked, stopping again and turning with a distraught look on her fine features.

How had I ever thought her nondescript?

"Not much like you. Mortality is all she would have in common with you."

"Sounds like you don't like her very much." Her curiosity bubbled below the surface, but I had to handle the conversation carefully.

"What she did to my father nearly killed him. He's not the same, and he never will be. We don't get along very well, but my heart does break for him. My mother was the absolute focal point in his life before he met his queen. His transformation was abrupt and complete, from moon to sun. He loved the new woman with everything in him and would have done anything to keep her happy, but there was one thing she wanted that he couldn't give her. I guess she wanted that more than a life with the King of Fairies."

"What did she want?" Lily breathed. I could see the wheels turning and wondered if she was thinking of things she would want more than me.

"A child." My voice was a curt whisper, and I gauged Lily's reaction carefully.

"Couldn't they adopt?"

"That wasn't much of a solution at the time," I informed her. "Adoption wasn't openly accepted. Besides, I think Guin—I think she wanted a child of her own, so when she met another human that she could have feelings for, she left my father."

I paused, thinking of a past that was almost too painful to remember. "I've certainly wondered if perhaps she was faithless, or maybe she didn't know what love was. I'm sure my father likes to think she truly loved him. He wants more than anything to believe that she would have stayed with him if he could have given her a child."

"I don't understand why he couldn't give her a child, anyway. He had you, didn't he?"

"It works differently between mortal and immortal," I said.

She blushed, amusing me thoroughly.

"Oh."

"Right. Oh." I nudged her playfully. "So, to answer your question, my father will most likely not like you. Can you handle that?"

"I can handle anything for you."

"I'm glad you said that, because our means of travel will probably scare the life out of you."

"Um," she laughed. "Don't put too much on me at once, now, okay?"

"You handle all of this very well," I complimented.

"Someday, there will be one thing that's too much to take. I'm not sure how I believe it all now. I'm constantly pinching myself to make sure I'm not dreaming. Apparently, I'm not. I wake up with massive bruises on my arms every morning, so I know the day before wasn't a dream, either."

I stared at her, horrified. "Don't hurt yourself like that."

She giggled. "I don't really pinch myself. It's just a saying. I mean that it's hard to accept sometimes that this is all real. I feel like the same person, but I know that I've truly been transformed. And I change more every day. I smiled at my mom this morning. Smiled at her! She looked like she might pass out. I think she wanted to check to see if I had a fever."

I laughed with her, but I could see the changes in Lily as well. Dave had recently commented on how happy she appeared, how open and playful she had been of late.

"But anyway, how do we travel? Are you going to sprinkle fairy dust on me and make me think happy thoughts?"

"Would you stop with the Tinkerbell?" I growled playfully, burying my face in her neck.

She threw her head back and laughed until her knees went weak. Just as when she sang, her mask was completely removed, and her heart was open wide.

"Okay, but seriously," she said, trying to catch a breath. "Are we flying?"

"Not today," I said snippily. "We're going to kind of disappear here and reappear at my father's house."

Lily's knees gave out, and she collapsed to the ground in another shower of giggles. I watched her through narrowed eyes as she rolled onto her back and crossed her arms over her stomach. "Oh, my God. I'm going to teleport. I wish I were in high school again so I could write a paper on what I did on my summer break. I know it would be better than any old 'went to the beach' essay. Teleporting!"

"Yes. That's what you call it." I watched her in consternation, fighting the grin that tugged at my lips. "You're hurting my feelings, love."

"Hem..." She sat up and cleared her throat. Her cheeks were flushed, and her eyes danced merrily. "Sorry. It's the only reaction I could think of. Teleporting."

Again, she was off, holding her stomach as she shrieked. I sighed, picked her up gently, and took a deep breath. With a quick turn on the spot, we vanished.

A CUIG DEAG

"Wow, " Lily whispered. "Where are we?"

"We're, um, under the Hill of Tara," I answered, setting her down.

I watched for her reactions. Her hand was still at the back of my neck, and it was quite a stretch for her. She didn't want to let go, so I reached up and took her fingers in mine.

"What do you call this place?" She continued to speak in hushed tones, and I felt a rush of affection for her.

"It's had several names over the centuries. Probably the most famous one would be *Tír na nÓg.* You've heard that one, right?"

She nodded, grinning, as she took in the wide, cobbled streets, lined with gas lamps that cast unusual shadows. The windows of several stone houses glowed with light from within. I could see how Lily might find my home city charming.

"So this is where you're *really* from." She peeked around me to gape at several people who strolled down the walk.

"It's where I've reluctantly called home for several hundred years, yes," I conceded with a nod.

I pushed her along because the few fairies that had been walking and minding their own business developed a sudden interest in us. A small crowd gathered, whispering with excitement.

"Is that for you or me?" she wondered nervously.

"It's for me," I assured her. The last thing she needed to think was that she couldn't be a normal human amongst a group of ethereal beings. "I'm the prince, you know."

"Oh, right. You don't seem like a prince to me." She allowed me to lead her down the street.

"You don't seem much like the daughter of a world-famous opera singer, either," I retorted.

"Thank God," she muttered.

"My feelings exactly."

She changed the subject. "How big is this place?"

"There are about half a million of us here at any given time, I suppose."

"It's a major city," she exclaimed. She touched the stones of the buildings in reverence, as she had the walls in Cratloe Castle.

"It is quite large. I'm not here much anymore. Don't you think it's dark? And kind of dirty?" My nose wrinkled in distaste as I took in the familiar surroundings.

Lily scanned the air above her, chuckling when she realized the sky wasn't visible. "It's hard to remember I'm underground. In fact, it's more like time travel. No cars. It doesn't look like there's any electricity. Am I right?"

"No, we've adopted the use of electricity, but cars would be impossible. Exhaust would destroy us. Besides, as you've seen, we've no need for them."

"Will we not suffocate eventually?" Lily wondered.

"No, love. We have excellent ventilation. That's the least of your worries here."

"The greatest being your father?"

"Very astute of you."

140

We were nearing the palace, and the anxiety of what was to come sent my pulse soaring. I couldn't remember what had possessed me to invite her into my personal hell, but to have any kind of future with her, I had to follow through with the present plans.

"Before I show you my house, perhaps you'd like to meet some of my friends?" I asked. I was stalling, but Lily didn't seem to mind. I pulled her to a small door and rapped the doorknocker.

When the door opened, Lily swayed on her feet in surprise. A tiny woman with immaculate features and hair almost as fiery as Lily's welcomed us in with excited gestures.

"Airdin, it's lovely to see you again. May I present Miss Lily Murphy? Lily, this is my dear friend, Airdin."

"So lovely to meet you, Lily." Airdin danced across the room and beckoned for us to follow her.

"Beagán, Prince Rioghan has come to visit," she called over her shoulder as she prepared a quick tea.

Lily wanted to ask many questions but politeness dictated she bite her tongue. Airdin was no more than three feet tall, and the man who joined us moments later was mere inches taller. He was also beautiful, in his own way. His tiny face was finely sculpted, and his hair a brilliant mop of shining gold.

"Did your lady-friend like the necklace, Master Rioghan?" Beagán asked.

My face heated with embarrassment that I had not given the choker to Lily as originally planned.

"You made that?" Lily whispered.

She looked at the small gentleman in front of her, and then cut her glare to me accusingly. She was once again angry that I'd wasted such a treasure on her mother. I still couldn't regret it, because I had saved Lily a great deal of trouble that day.

"It is one of the most beautiful things I've ever seen," she said, addressing Beagán again.

He basked in her praise, and I was grateful she hadn't given away my secret. We chatted easily with my little friends, but we needed to fulfill our intentions for the trip.

With deep regret, we said our goodbyes. Airdin dabbed at her eyes with a dainty handkerchief as Lily placed a kiss on her smooth cheek. Beagán blushed a deep red when he received his own buss. When the door shut behind us, Lily turned to me.

"Leprechauns?" she asked.

I nodded, and she swayed unsteadily again.

"You let me know when it gets to be too much," I warned her. "I may get carried away, but I enjoy sharing this with you."

"If I reach my breaking point, you'll be the first to know." Lily laughed.

We neared the palace, and I found it hard to share her amusement. Her breath caught, and I turned to assure her safety. She stood in reverence, a hand over her heart. The home I took for granted was an astonishing sight.

The walls of our great fortress towered above us, made of the very same stone that covered the courtyard in which we stood. Cut-crystal windows sparkled with light from the chandeliers that hung in each chamber, and the servant quarters to the left were almost as impressive as the main house. Underground waterfalls cascaded in the background. The roar of the falls did not mask her amazed murmurs as she inspected the sparkling rivers that flowed on either side of us. Lanterns lining the walkways reflected against the water and the quartz in the stone, creating the illusion that we stood among millions of diamonds.

She gazed at the twenty-foot wooden doors in front of us. I took a deep breath and pulled the handle. We stepped into entrance hall, and Lily gasped again. An enormous crystal chandelier hung over our heads, stairs of the finest Connemara marble curved gracefully to a second floor, vases of solid gold held roses of brilliant hues, and a brightly woven rug softened the sounds of our footsteps over the ancient stone.

Lily, rather than gush over the opulence, walked straight to the wall lined with portraits of my father and me.

"Your hair was so long." She studied my favorite, her eyes wide.

"It was the style of the time." I ducked my head to hide my embarrassment.

"I guess this is the closest I could ever get to seeing baby pictures of you," she teased.

"It is rather uncomfortable," I acknowledged.

She walked slowly down the hallway, taking in each painting with a delighted smile. "Where's your room?"

"It's further back. I'll show you that first."

I hadn't seen any of the staff. It was disconcerting, because I knew my father was aware of our presence. Nothing missed his watchful eye. I thought perhaps he was preparing our ejection from the castle. I pulled Lily into my chambers and shut the door. She didn't miss my swift movements and turned to me with a quizzical look.

Her eyes hungrily wandered over my belongings. I could almost see the wheels turning as she tried to gain insight into my life from my possessions.

The bed stood on a platform in the center of the room. Heavy, dark quilts covered the mattresses, and they matched the drapes that hung from the ceiling. An enormous wardrobe with beveled mirrors covered one wall, reflecting her wondrous expression.

"It's so clean," she said, her words a mild accusation.

I shrugged. "I don't live here anymore. Plus, the staff will make sure to erase any sign of our visit."

Feeling rebellious, I pushed my fist into a pillow, creating a crater. I immediately felt guilty about creating extra work for the staff. It was their job to ensure that everything remained in place.

"You're a bad influence on me." I sighed as I licked my finger and ran it down the middle of the wardrobe mirror.

"Your room is your prison, isn't it?" Though she phrased it as a question, I knew she wasn't asking. She had me figured out.

"More than you know." I pulled her close and buried my nose in her hair to just breathe for a moment. "We should probably just go see Father and get out of here. I'm starting to get the creeps."

"I've had them since we walked in," she admitted, shivering.

I led her out of the room and down the hall to the throne-room. Father would be there, especially since Lily was with me. It gave him a powerful air, and he would count on all the intimidation possible when dealing with us.

I didn't knock. It was a habit I had developed years ago, feeling the Crown Prince shouldn't need to. We were only a few steps into the room when Father spoke.

"I find it nearly impossible to believe that you've brought her here." Ailbhe's voice was cold.

"Only nearly?" I tried to downplay his rudeness for Lily's sake.

"You are you, and you will constantly defy me. Never mind the fact that no human eyes have ever touched upon our home here. Never mind that she has already seen entirely too much anyway. It was very irresponsible of you. Now I shall have to think long and hard about the consequences of this new development."

"I'm very sorry to have upset you, Your Highness." Lily's voice held meekness I'd never heard from her.

She edged farther behind me, her expression begging for my protection. I smiled at her warmly, letting her know she had nothing to fear.

"I wanted you to meet her, Father. You are both important parts of my life, and I can't bear the thought of not being able to join the two."

"Out of the question," Ailbhe snarled. "She can never be a part of your world. Do you not understand that this life is unchanging for us? And yet, for her, every day is change. She ages each second that she stands here. Does this mean nothing to you?"

"It doesn't," I said, shrugging. "I love her anyway."

"You can't understand." Ailbhe heaved a great breath of frustration and sadness. "You're only a boy in so many ways. You have so much to learn before you'll be ready to take over the ruling of the kingdom."

"You know I don't want to rule the kingdom." Irritation began to curl through my stomach, but I refrained from stomping my foot like a child.

"Yes, you want to be a little boy and have fun forever and ever," Ailbhe spat. "What a disappointment you are."

"Nice. Every son wants to hear that, don't they?"

Lily put her hand on my arm, and the anger and tension drained from me.

"It's not as bad as it sounds," she whispered. "Wouldn't you rather be a disappointment to one and a delight to everyone else? I know I would."

"Thank you, stupid human, for proving how mismatched you are. My son is a prince and should think as a prince. He must carry with him the wisdom of the ages so he can make intelligent and well-formed decisions. You are the latest in a long line of ill-conceived ideas. Don't expect to last. He bores easily."

To me, he said, "There will be serious repercussions for this. I honestly have no idea how to deal with your insolence. I can only beg you to rethink your hasty decisions. Don't give up your birthright for a filthy human."

With that, we were both dismissed. I gave Lily an embarrassed shrug. I had known it wouldn't go well but hadn't expected such horrible insults from the man who called himself a king. She smiled reassuringly and patted my arm as we hurried back the way we had come.

"Parents suck sometimes," she whispered.

I wrapped an arm around her shoulders and pulled her close. Nuzzling my nose above her ear, I whispered, "Thank you."

We stepped outside, and she flinched.

"You all right, love?"

"I expected daylight. I forgot we were underground for a minute."

"It does take some getting used to. You should better prepare yourself for the journey this time," I warned her as I shut the palace door behind us.

Her eyes danced with laughter, but she bit her lip to keep from chuckling aloud.

"Deep breath now."

She complied, and a moment later we were back on the hillside next to Cratloe Castle.

A SE ÒEAG

"So that was Father. He's never been the same since we were lost. Mother wasn't with us that day, so…"

We sat in a small pub on Barrack's Street. After our return from *Tír na nÓg*, we had driven back to town and checked on Aisling at the hotel. She and Ciarán were at an outdoor cafe, and Lily had given them both hugs. She'd barely said a word to me as we walked out of City Center toward Dirty Nancy's. I felt compelled to break the silence after we had our pints in front of us, and my opening worked.

"So you were born? Like, how a human is born?" Lily interrupted, her face alight with curiosity. Her hunger for knowledge was matched only by my desire to share everything I possibly could.

"Nothing quite so bloody and painful as that, no. But I am the product of love." I smiled at her confusion.

"But how does that happen? I mean, you know. Angels having sex?"

"Come on, Lily. Do you think humans are the only beings permitted to engage in an act of love? With my parents, it was

147

more than that. It was completely pure, the way it was intended to be."

"And then what happened?" She leaned forward over the table, pushing her cider away so that her view of me was unobstructed.

"I just became." I struggled to find words to explain my existence. It wasn't something I had ever needed to describe before.

"So your mother didn't carry you for nine months and then go through agony in some heavenly hospital room with clouds and harps and things?"

"You amuse me with your vision of Heaven. Why does everyone think Heaven is in the sky? It's not something you could look for. You can't get in a spaceship and travel to Heaven. It's like… How would you describe it? A whole different dimension. Another world that doesn't exist in this time and place. And before you can ask, Hell is not the center of the Earth."

"That one I can comprehend," she muttered. "But you've changed the subject."

"I don't know how to describe it. My father loved my mother, and I began to exist."

"Just like this? A full-grown man? Er, fairy?"

"Well, no. This is my earthly form. As an angel, I was just there…light, sound, smell. I remember my mother the most clearly. To survive Earth's atmosphere, we must have a human form. I can appear as I choose."

"Wait." She struggled with her next words. "You don't look like this? Like this beautiful, blue-eyed god?"

"I do." I was secretly thrilled by her description of me as beautiful. "This is my true earthly form, the form I chose for my visits."

"Lucky. So I get that Heaven isn't some cloudy paradise."

"Oh, it's paradise," I interrupted.

She waved her hand impatiently. "I get that part. What I don't get is you appearing out of nowhere. Your mother didn't give birth to you?"

"Lily," I began. "When Eve ate of the fruit, she doomed women forever to the pain of childbirth."

"There was an apple?" Lily demanded, her face full of incredulity.

"Symbolic." I shrugged. "This fruit of knowledge was the discovery of lust. She seduced Adam, turning a beautiful act into a sordid one. This is why they were at once aware of their nakedness and sought to hide it from one another, and God, in his infinite mercy and wisdom, chose to turn this ugly act into something miraculous. Eve could now become a mother, but not without the pain to remind her of her sin."

She arched an eyebrow and I accepted her unspoken statement. With my cavalier past, of which she knew only little, I could be thought quite the hypocrite.

"Please remember I don't necessarily hold these beliefs. I may have at one point, but I've been on Earth far too long, with far too many temptations. Even knowing the history, understanding the beginning, I'm not without desires."

"Fair enough. It's all just so…wild. I heard all this stuff in movies or read it in books, and it's true, or close to true. I always figured it was an apple. Or some prehistoric fruit that doesn't exist anymore."

"You would be surprised how much of mythology is based on actual events. The story has to start somewhere."

"Point taken," Lily murmured. "Were you there? I mean, were you alive?"

"I was. We were very unhappy with the newcomers."

"You mean the humans?" Lily asked, a scowl crossing her lovely features.

"Precisely."

"Are you planning to tell me why?"

"Maybe another time."

She had far too much to process, and I wasn't sure how much she could handle at one time. The frown on her face told me in no uncertain terms that she would not be letting the subject go.

"Later, Lily," I warned. "I've told you so much already. Did you know I used to keep a journal? I've stopped writing since telling you my stories, but I have tens of thousands of books with all of my thoughts since writing began. Someday you can read them all to your heart's content, but for now, it's just too much."

She heaved a giant sigh and grabbed my hand. "Let's pick up Aisling from the hotel and go to Cobh."

"What's there?" I asked, surprise coloring my voice.

"History," was her cryptic answer.

I shrugged once and allowed her to lead me to the car.

*

I quite liked Aisling; don't get me wrong. She was a very sweet girl, and I loved how Lily always smiled when her new friend was around. Some might think that I didn't want to share, but that's not true. Perhaps it was because I could be my real self with Lily but always had to watch what I said or did when others were around.

I had to bite my tongue so as not to give away too much information the whole time we were in Cobh. Of course, I had known many of the emigrants who sailed from that very port over a hundred years before, and I certainly remembered when the Titanic sank. I clamped my lips shut as we wandered through the museum, wanting desperately to share some of my own experiences with Lily. As the girls walked on ahead, I stared at an exhibit featuring the prisoner ships that sailed to Australia. It was an eerily familiar sight, and before I could stop it, the past came rushing back in a jumbled memory.

Lily was not the first human I had befriended. There had been many during my thousands of years of life, though Lily was the first I had given my heart to. There had been a boy once. His name was Michael, and he had been about ten years of age when we met.

I lived in Dublin at the time, probably 1790, and it was a city of many contradictions. The rich Englishmen walked by the poor, content in their possessions and ignoring those less fortunate. They would go to their well-appointed homes, while thousands of men, women, and children shivered on the streets and scrounged through rubbish for something to fill their aching bellies. Little Michael refused to let his status get him down. I first spotted him outside my house where he sat on a wooden crate. He had waved happily when he saw me.

"Hiya, mister. That sure is a nice coat," he said.

"Thank you, kindly," I replied, smiling at him absently.

I had more on my mind at the time. I'd had an argument with my father about how we might be able to help the starving people of our country. He wanted nothing of it, for he ached over the loss of his first love since my mother. Humans held no sway over him anymore; not since Guinevere's betrayal. Seeing that little boy, who was so thin that his bones nearly jutted through his skin, made me ache with sadness for him.

"Can I get you something to eat?" I asked. His eyes lit up, but quickly thereafter his face fell.

"No, thank you, sir." He sounded as if it almost killed him to say, and my curiosity was aroused.

"Whyever not?" I demanded. My tone was harsher than I'd intended, not with irritation for him but rather his situation.

"Because you have earned what you will eat," he said, his voice so soft I almost couldn't hear.

"I see," I said thoughtfully. He was a boy with a conscience, and my heart went out to him.

"Perhaps if you earned what you will eat?" I offered. His face lit up again, and he nodded. "I have many tasks around the house that you could help me with."

"Could I perhaps do twice the work and take some food to my sister, Mary?" he asked, his eyes wide and innocent.

"You can, of course."

And so it went that every day he would wait outside of my house until I arrived in the evenings. I would create some tasks for him to do, and he would take home great chunks of bread, cheese, meat, and flasks of clean drinking water for himself and his sister. I grew to love the little boy, and I was sure he had grown attached to me. Often after he cleaned and before he left with his earnings, he would sit with me in front of the fire and listen as I told "fairy tales" about my family. He grew ever more healthy, with roses coloring his cheeks and a bright sparkle ornamenting his wide blue eyes. I knew he depended on me, so what I did was unforgivable. I told myself often that I had only been acting out of concern for my little friend, but there were other ways I could have been of use.

I went home to *Tír na nÓg* to try to reason with my father once more. He would still hear nothing of it and even went so far as to have me banished from the castle. While I argued with the guards in the Otherworld, little Michael sat on my doorstep crying. He thought I had forgotten him, so what he did next was understandable. He stole a loaf of bread that had been cooling in a window. I was rushing home at the time and caught him in the act.

"Please, Mr. Rioghan. My sister is so sick and she only gets better when she has food in her belly. Please don't be angry at me."

"Of course I'm not angry at you, child. Hand me the bread so we may return it."

He did as he was told as the gardaí rounded the corner.

"Thief," they cried, converging on little Michael.

His tears began again, and his frail shoulders shook. He counted on me to be home so that he could feed his sister. Mary would surely die without him to provide for her.

"He is nothing of the sort," I said. "You'll not arrest this boy, because he is innocent. I stole the loaf of bread to give to him."

Three sets of eyes looked at me in disbelief. I, with my expensive clothing and shoes, was a thief? Rather than argue the point, they shooed Michael away and snapped shackles on my wrists.

"May I say goodbye to my friend?" I asked politely.

The guards stepped back and allowed me a moment. I leaned forward to Michael and whispered, "Take the key from my coat pocket. You and your family may live in my home until I return. And I will return. Just make sure it's kept tidy for me, and you will earn your keep, my man."

Michael's fingers trembled as he reached into my pocket. He palmed the key expertly, indicating he'd done his share of thievery. I winked and set him on his way.

Escaping would have been easy, except I was constantly under supervision. The trial was something of a joke, where hundreds of criminals were herded together and sentenced jointly to the penal colony in Australia. We all waited together in a stinking cell, where my expensive clothes were and I was given rags to wear. After two weeks, we crammed into a prison ship, departed from Queenstown, and the longest journey of my life began.

Three months on open water with thieves, rapists, and murderers vomiting from seasickness, crying to God, fighting amongst themselves, and eventually accepting their fate. I sat silently, waiting for the first moment when I was alone so I could return to Ireland and make sure Michael and Mary had followed my instructions. I had scarcely touched the soil of New South Wales when my moment arrived.

The shackles were removed from my wrists and feet, and I was instructed to follow a small group of men. I started in that direction, but broke away once I was within running distance of a small copse of trees. I reached it before anyone even shouted for me to stop and, taking a deep breath, I vanished. I reappeared only a moment later in the back garden at my Dublin home, lungs bursting with the need for oxygen. I had never attempted such a long distance of travel before and hadn't adequately prepared for it.

The lights were burning cheerily in my pantry, and I could hear childish laughter, making my heart swell. My friend would be there to greet me. I knocked on the back door and held my arms out to Michael when he opened the door.

"Rioghan! I told Mary ye'd make it."

He dragged me inside, and I was finally able to meet the small girl that occupied the largest part of Michael's heart. Her ruined feet were propped in front of her, but her smile told me that she did not let them bother her.

It wasn't easy to heal her illness because no one knew what it was. I worked at it every night, and she was eventually as whole and healthy as her brother. As advances in medicine were made, I learned that she had been afflicted with juvenile diabetes. At that moment, her cheeks had been as rosy and as full as Michael's, and I knew in an instant that I would provide for them as long as I could, damn what my father said.

On one occasion, I did happen upon a man that had arrested me in that alleyway. He stopped dead in the street and stared at me for a full minute before shaking his head and deciding that he must be going crazy. I laughed all the way home, sharing the story with my "children" when I arrived.

"Are you alright, love?" Lily's voice intruded on my thoughts.

I shook off the memories and forced a smile. "Just remembering an old friend."

Her eyes widened, and her expression said I would be sharing later. I laughed and nodded as she laced her fingers through mine and dragged me forward to meet up with Aisling, who was looking at a bright red jumper with particular interest.

"You'd look lovely in that sweater," Lily told her as we approached.

The gift shop was nearly empty, and the lone employee hoped for a last-minute sale before the museum closed.

"I couldn't." Aisling's cheeks turned the same shade of red as the coveted jumper.

"Not only could you, you should," Lily prodded. She took the clothing from the hanger and held it up to Aisling, nodding at the way the color brightened her friend's pale countenance. "Oh, yes. This sweater is a must, isn't it, Rioghan?"

I tried to look properly excited, but clothes shopping was definitely something that should stay between girls.

"It looks nice," I said sincerely.

Lily thunked the jumper down onto the counter.

"I'll have this and those red earrings." Lily pointed at a delicate silver pair, with red stones in the form of tiny flowers.

"Lily, stop." Aisling hid her face in her hands.

"I won't. They'll be perfect. You can wear them tonight when we go to eat. You are coming, right?"

Aisling meekly accepted the bag of purchases with a small smile. "Thank you. I don't know what I did before I met you, Lily."

"That's funny," I remarked. "I can't quite remember, either."

It was Lily's turn to blush furiously, and I laughed as she dragged us from the shop. Aisling even offered up a giggle at Lily's expense.

a seacht deag

"So, I think you should tell me who it was your father fell in love with," Lily said.

Her voice surprised me out of my daydream. I had been picturing a house on a cliff in the West of Ireland, made of stone and mortar, with a stone wall surrounding the front garden and a view of the ocean in the back. There would be a cozy couch in front of a large fireplace, where Lily would lay with her head in my lap and sing to me.

"Rioghan?" she said. "Did you hear me?"

"Sorry, love. I was daydreaming."

"Apparently." She grinned. "I wondered if you'd tell me more about your father's human love. I mean, apparently this is a battle I'll have to fight for the rest of my life. I guess I'd like to know what I'm fighting against."

"You've thought about this a lot, have you?" I curled my fingers through hers.

"Only constantly."

"Let's review, shall we?" I suggested, as a teacher would.

"You think I'm still not ready for new information?" Her face showed her understanding, and in that moment I knew that she was, in fact, ready.

"Actually, I think you are."

"Yeah? Cool." She plopped down on the bench next to me, crossed her legs, and propped her chin in her hand.

"Again, I have no proof to offer you that will support what I'm about to tell you," I warned.

She waved her hand in a "get on with it" gesture and smiled. "I don't need proof from you anymore."

"This happened so long ago, Lily. You must understand I can tell you many, many times I've been here since the beginning of the Earth, but when I tell you this story, you'll still feel inclined to disbelieve it."

"I'm still wrapping my head around everything, no doubt," Lily acknowledged. "But I want to know. I want to hear everything you can tell me."

"All right. We'll give this a try, then."

"Look, Rioghan. You've told me that you're an angel on Earth. You've met Lucifer; your father is King of the Fairies. Whatever you tell me will be filed away under true fairy tales, and I'll sift through it as I'm able."

"My father married a woman named Guinevere," I started. I had been mulling in my mind how to broach the subject, and that was what came rushing forth.

"I only know of one Guinevere in history," Lily said with a frown. "The one married to…"

"King Arthur, yes," I finished. I watched her face, but it was blank.

"She left your father for King Arthur?" she finally asked.

I hesitated a moment before answering. "Not exactly."

"You're not making much sense," she said, flinging her legs over the arm of the bench.

She laid her head in my lap, as she had done in my daydream. As I watched her curls spread over my legs, I couldn't help but lose myself again in reverie.

Lily was silent as I ran my fingers through her silken strands. Her brow creased as she worked through the facts in her head, so I let her continue to ponder. Instead of speaking, I brushed my thumbs over her temples. It was tempting to show her, but no. She had too much to process.

"Can I...?" I started, but she sat up and cut me off mid-sentence.

"Your father is King Arthur?" she shrieked. "Is that what you're trying to say? That your father is King Arthur, and I visited Avalon? King Arthur didn't die?"

"Ah..." I stuttered.

She did exactly as I'd hoped and guessed what I was trying to tell her. Once she knew, I had trouble filling in the gaps. There was so much to the story. How could I put so much love, devotion, sacrifice, betrayal, brokenness, and hate into words?

"Am I right?" Lily demanded. "Is that what happened?"

I had been silent for almost a full minute as I tried to decide how best to continue. "I'd like to show you, if I could?"

"What do you mean, show me?" Her eyes were wide, but there was still no fear.

"I can show you my memories, if you'll let me," I explained. "It will feel to you as if you're there. Would you like to see it that way, or would you prefer I tell you the story?"

"Can I choose to see it through your eyes and then change my mind if it's too weird?" she asked, her eyes flashing with interest.

"Of course. Just tell me if it's too much. I can stop at any time."

"Then go for it." She looked so excited I almost wanted to laugh.

"All right. I think it was about the sixth century, but the years do melt together. We were in England, and my father was a friend to humans. He had accepted their request for help with the Saxon invaders. To his subjects, he was invincible."

"Well, he's immortal, right?" Lily interrupted.

"Of course. But how do you tell humans that without scaring them? The land now known as Great Britain and Ireland was still what we call pagan today, but beliefs were beginning to change. In some areas of the world, supernatural happenings spurred cries of witchcraft or pacts with Satan."

"So he was human, as far as anyone knew?"

"That was all he could be. So, now you know the background. I'll show you the day he met Guinevere and go from there, okay?"

"I'm ready." Her eyes were closed dreamily, and I caressed her cheek before placing my fingers at her temples. She jumped when she saw the first of my memories.

I sat on a stool next to a roaring fire. Mordred glowered in the corner, working at a piece of wood with his knife. Father was at the head of the table, eating what appeared to be a whole chicken. Because the language at that time would be unintelligible to Lily, I tried my hardest to translate my memories for her sake.

"The people would like to see me take a queen," Father announced.

Mordred glowered still more, and I shrugged.

"I imagine I can keep up appearances for some time. A Welsh girl, I think, will be arriving momentarily. I expect you to be polite and keep your mouths shut."

I was indifferent to the turn of events. Father wasn't the purest of souls. He often took a lover to erase memories of my mother. The fact that one of these lovers would be around more than a week or so was not something terribly interesting to me.

At that moment, the chamber door opened and Gawain and Gareth entered. Following them was one of the most beautiful humans I had ever seen. In fact, she was so flawless that I was tempted to believe that there was more to her than met the eye. Her skin was cream and roses, her eyes deep pools of brightest blue. A patrician nose attested to her noble birth, and dusky pink lips were curved into a warm smile.

"My king," she said, dipping into a deep curtsy.

Father stood, his chair scraping the stone floor, and I followed suit. Mordred stayed hidden in the shadows with a severe frown. He could always be counted on for his rudeness.

"Guinevere," my father cried, stepping forward to take her hands.

It was the first time he had laid eyes on her, and he was not disappointed. He was smitten from that very moment. Pretending to love his queen would not be a tall order.

"Please meet Mordred and Amr, my sons."

"Wait." Lily interrupted her vision.

"Too much?" I asked, brushing the hair back from her face.

"No. This is amazing. I want to know why he called you Amr. I've never even heard the name Amr, but I've heard of everyone else, so far."

"Rioghan hasn't always been my name. I've had several over the millennia, and Amr was one. You've not heard of me because we tried very hard to avoid notoriety. Ending up in the history books, even as a legend, was not something my father ever intended. I suppose I managed to behave myself better than everyone else."

"How were you able to slip into oblivion when your father and brother were so well known?" she persisted.

"Do you want me to tell you the story, or shall I continue sharing history as I remember it?"

"Oh." She grinned bashfully. "Sorry. I want to see."

I placed my fingers at her temples and continued to give her my memories.

"I'm so pleased to meet you both," Guinevere said. She gave a deep curtsy to the three of us.

The next month was a flurry of activity in my memory. There were specific moments I remembered very clearly, such as the first time I realized my father was truly in love with Guinevere. I could also recall, in detail, the wedding day.

After the wedding, two major events stuck out in my memory, the day I walked in on Mordred attempting to seduce Guinevere and the day that Lancelot arrived. Both days stood out as times I should have sensed Guinevere's faithless nature.

In the matter of Mordred's failed amorous advances, I could forgive her. She was new to the castle, to the family, and was constantly kept in the dark about our abilities and origins.

"Wait," Lily interrupted again.

"You have a question?" I felt a surge of affection and pressed a kiss to her fingers. Of course my girl would have a question.

Her eyes were open again, searching mine for answers.

"Was Mordred your full brother? You share the same mother?"

"No. He was a half-brother. His mother was Morgause, another fairy."

"So, your dad only loved two, but he slept with more?" she guessed. Her brow was wrinkled in confusion.

"Mmhmm," I murmured. "This is true. However, in the case of Mordred, Father was kind of tricked. Morgause waited until he was drunk before seducing him."

"So alcohol affects you?" Lily jumped right on that tidbit.

"It does. Anything that affects a human can affect us. We have the ability to heal. Therefore, a drunken state does not last as long."

"I bet you don't get a hangover, either," Lily groused. I chuckled and shook my head. "That's completely unfair."

"Many of us might be tempted to argue that with you," I countered, "but that's off the current topic. Would you prefer to follow this new path of discussion, or would you like to finish the memories of Guinevere?"

"Guinevere, please." She crossed her hands primly over her stomach and affected a look of absolute innocence. "I won't interrupt anymore. Okay, I can't promise that, but I'll try not to change the subject anymore, at least."

"Fair enough," I conceded.

Father allowed Guinevere to share every aspect of his life. I didn't know when he shared our family secret with her, but it became clear he didn't intend to keep anything from her. She was given a seat at the knights' table, awarded the power to hand out orders, and very nearly became something of a mother to me. I was inordinately fond of her, and we often took walks to discuss life, battle strategy, and her desire for a child.

At the time, I didn't understand what could happen if a human woman attempted to bear an immortal child. My father was against the possibility, and he was more knowledgeable. I suggested she approach him for the reasoning behind his decisions and spawned the first of our family feuds.

Father was enraged that I had dared speak to his wife of things that were "none of my concern," as he had phrased it. To Guinevere, he insisted the closeness she and I shared must stop. Mordred sat by and laughed at the whole situation, making snide comments about stealing my father's wife when I was within earshot.

Guinevere grew to fear her husband—my father—and his temper. I wanted to reassure her that he loved her above all else, but I was allowed no opportunity. Instead, I had to watch as her fear turned to terror and then despair. She felt like a prisoner in her own home, and I had no idea what I could do to make things easier for her.

We all believed things could not get any more uncomfortable, and then Lancelot arrived. He was a breath of fresh air, with his bawdy laugh and terrific stories. My father was quite taken with his new friend and invited him to join the rest of the knights.

Lancelot, true to all the legends, was a fighter of great skill. He led several battles for my father, returning the victor each time. He became almost as much a hero of the people as my father. Arthur, at that time, was a very generous king and happily shared the glory with Lancelot. Within a few short months, Lancelot found his way to the head of the table.

While we were distracted by his heroic deeds, he found his way into Guinevere's heart. We never knew if she shared the circumstances of our existence. It seems silly to describe the situation as "here one minute, gone the next," but that was exactly what happened.

Lancelot returned one evening from a victorious battle and received the welcome of a favored son. A feast was given in his honor, and he sat beside my father for the first time. Mordred was livid at his removal from the right hand of King Arthur. I, however, had seen my seat taken with the arrival of our lovely queen and felt no qualms at the turn of events.

We all celebrated early into the morning before stumbling to our chambers to sleep. When we awoke the next morning, Guinevere and Lancelot were gone. There was no indication as to the how or why, but my father knew. Guinevere had been presented with an acceptable offer, and she had taken it.

From that point on, Father changed. The rift between us grew exponentially with each passing year. Mordred began to take advantage of the king's despondency, eventually betraying him— his own father—at the Battle of Camlann. Arthur managed to kill Mordred in the battle and decided it was time to retire from human view.

And so Father crossed the sea to Avalon. My aunt, Father's sister, Morgan le Fay, carried him and helped him heal. He retained his title as the King of Fairies with the help of Morgan and has remained there since.

"Are you telling me I visited Avalon?" Lily asked in a hushed whisper.

"Well, of course," I answered her with a wink. "Ireland itself is Avalon."

"But I thought… What about Glastonbury?" Lily stuttered.

"Ah, well. That was some trickery, wasn't it?" I said sheepishly. "We can't have anyone figuring out what happened to King Arthur, can we?"

"And Excalibur?" Lily asked.

"Was used to kill Mordred, yes."

"Even though Mordred was a fairy? I thought you couldn't die," she said, clenching her fists in agitated confusion.

"You caught that, did you? This is why Father was given Excalibur. Vivianne knew he would need it."

"And who the hell is Vivianne?" Lily grew more frustrated with each of my answers, as I knew she would.

"She's another sprite, like Merlin." I knew I was driving her crazy, but I couldn't help spurring her on with my short and succinct answers.

"You keep saying all of this like *everybody* knows it," she wailed. "I have more questions now than before you started the story."

"Typical," I said wryly.

"What's so special about Merlin and Vivianne? What can they do that you can't?"

"It's hard to explain," I started.

"Try," Lily said grimly, but a smile still pulled at the corners of her mouth.

"Time has no meaning to them. They live in past, present, and future. They're aware of all things at all times. That's how Vivianne knew to make sure Arthur had Excalibur."

"So Vivianne is the Lady of the Lake, right?" Lily clarified.

"Right."

"And the sword in the stone? What about that? Didn't your dad pull the sword out of some stone somewhere?"

"Nope. Classic misinterpretation through the centuries. It's the sword *of* stone, not the sword *in* the stone."

"I should write a book," Lily mumbled. "I'd make millions."

JENNIFER M. BARRY

a hocht deag

Lily seemed happy enough as she sat with Aisling and sipped her coffee. We were in Dublin again so Celia could meet with a casting director. Lily was both amused and disgusted that Celia was being considered for the role of doting mother on a new Irish sitcom.

I placed a quick kiss against Lily's temple and waved to her companions.

We had already discussed plans to visit my father, and I knew she wasn't excited about repeating her earlier experience. I thought it best if I made the trip alone. I felt the weight of dread crushing my shoulders as I trudged toward an alleyway. I was pretty sure it would be empty at that time of day so I could make my escape unnoticed.

The pressing trepidation didn't ease when I arrived in *Tír na nÓg*. In fact, it increased ten-fold. I held my head high and marched to the castle as I willed my pulse to slow to a normal speed. As expected, Ailbhe was waiting for me. How he always knew where I was or where I was going, I would never know. He spoke before I could open my mouth.

"Have you brought more filthy humans with you?" His voice was dangerously low.

"She's not filthy," I protested, taking the defensive immediately. That was not how I had planned to start the conversation. "She's a beautiful person. You've got to give her a chance, Father. I know you'd like her."

"You sound like a child," Ailbhe sniffed.

His words pulled me up short.

"I think I feel like one," I marveled. "But I've never been a child, so I'm not sure how one would feel and act."

"You know more about acting like a child than you think," he assured me snidely.

"Can you not find it in your heart to give her a chance?"

Without thinking, I approached his chair and sat at his feet. It was something I hadn't done in centuries, not since Guinevere had destroyed him. The same thought must have crossed his mind, because he lifted a hand to place it on my head. I could almost see the memories running through his mind. Moments later, he must have recalled her last moments with him, for he jerked his hand away from my hair as if I burned him.

"They are all the same, I'm afraid. You must leave behind the silly notion of loving a human. There is much you need to learn about the running of a kingdom."

"Father, being your heir is pointless. We're immortal. We don't die. Why would I train to take over a throne that will never be vacated?"

"You are aware it's not so much about taking over as it is about supporting me and the decisions that I make as king."

"But you've made these decisions for thousands of years, and I've never had anything to say about it. Why now?"

"I've indulged your silly whims for as long as I can. You've gone traipsing about the Earth, living like a spoiled child, or worse, a lottery winner. It's time for you to learn something about responsibility, about the kingdom."

"I don't want to be a king." I pressed my head back into his hand for reassurance.

"Really, Rioghan." Father sighed. "Must I pick another successor? Morrigan is more than willing."

"Really, Father," I mocked. "I would be much more comfortable if you did."

"Seems it would be easier to rid the world of the human girl," Father mused.

"You wouldn't." My voice was little more than a whisper as the cold hand of fear grabbed my heart and squeezed violently.

"As you are my heir, I will respect your wishes," Father said.

I heard the unspoken threat in his words. As long as I began to behave as a prince, left Lily behind, and took up my new role as heir to the throne, he would not harm her. If I found that impossible, Ailbhe would simply remove the problem.

"I honestly believe I can have both," I protested. "I'd like to show you that I'm capable."

"As you wish," Father said, dismissing me with a flick of his fingers.

My journey back to Dublin seemed to take hours, though it was little more than an instant. I trusted my father not to harm Lily, but there had been a seed of doubt planted during my visit. Just the thought of losing her made me tremble, but I had to believe that Ailbhe would eventually see reason. Still, I could not shake the fear.

Lily was standing outside the hotel when I returned. The dark cloud that had followed me from Tara to Dublin disappeared the moment I saw her laughing with Frankie, the tattered tinker. It never ceased to amaze me how loudly she made my heart sing.

"Where did Aisling go?" I asked as soon as I was within earshot.

"Shopping, if you can believe it." Lily giggled. "She said she'd be back soon and we could all go eat."

"Excellent. I'm starving. You'll join us, right?" I clapped my hands together and looked at Frankie expectantly.

"Oh, you'll not be wantin' me around." He started to back away, but Lily tucked her arm through his in a flash.

"We most certainly will be wantin' you around," she assured him. "Besides, I have yet to make it up to you for the way I behaved last time we saw each other."

"Tha's not necessary, love." Tears sparkled in his crinkly eyes, and pure love shone on his face as he looked at her.

I wondered who had last treated him with the same regard Lily did. He was probably more often ignored than not, and I would wager he had never been asked to dinner.

"That's what makes it so darn fun," Lily assured him. She waved at Aisling, who crossed the road with an armload of bags.

"Donovan Cole had a sale. I didn't know when to stop. It's been so long since I bought anything. And Frankie, wait until you see." She dropped all the bags, reminding me of the first time we had met, but her purchases stayed in the bags as she dug around in them.

"Here," she exclaimed in triumph.

In her hands was a brilliant plaid scarf, which she tenderly placed around Frankie's neck. He reached up with a trembling hand to smooth his hand over the soft wool.

"I know it's only August, and you don't need it during the day," Aisling began, staring to feel self-conscious.

"It's very much appreciated." His voice choked with emotion.

Tears that had been threatening started to spill. He looked at each of us in turn, his expression full of love and gratitude. The quiet grace that I glimpsed on his face was truly beautiful. I heard gasps from the girls, and I knew I wasn't the only one to see it.

"Come," I said, breaking the trance. "Let's find something to eat, shall we?"

I playfully looped Lily's arm through mine. Aisling tucked her hand through Frankie's elbow, and we set off for the café on the corner. Dave followed at a discreet distance and took a table across the room so that he could keep an eye on his charge.

Laughter was not in short supply during our late afternoon dinner. Frankie regaled us with tales of his adventures during his life on the streets, while Aisling complained about her nosy neighbor who was always banging on the apartment walls and asking if she had a man in there with her. Lily treated us to stories about her mother's infamous tantrums. I thought about the many stories that I could tell, but all would raise too many questions.

"Well, this is a cozy little scene," a voice drawled. I didn't even need to look up.

"Morrigan," I said curtly.

Frankie and Aisling stiffened, and I wondered if Morrigan seemed as evil to those who had never met her. She was, effectively, the Princess of Fairies, as she was my father's sister, and she played her role well. Her shining hair and flashing blue eyes could belong to no other being. To an experienced eye, she could be nothing but fairy.

"Is this the human that's causing such an uproar?" my aunt asked gleefully, fingering Lily's soft hair.

Morrigan's curls were in perfect order—a stark contrast to the wild abandon of Lily's tresses. Bile rose to my throat as Lily looked to me for reassurance. Her eyes skittered across the table to Frankie and Aisling. When she saw the same fear I did, her expression filled with trepidation.

"Your father is watching, Rioghan," Morrigan whispered directly into my ear. "As am I. You can either keep your little girl safe or your title. I'd prefer if you kept your girl, as it were."

"That's my intention," I snarled.

Dave watched intently, wondering if he needed to intervene. I shook my head to let him know that I had it well in hand.

"Yes. Ailbhe said you'd say that," Morrigan continued. "I don't think you're aware of the consequences, but that's all the better for me, isn't it?"

"If you'll excuse us, Auntie Morrigan," I said with saccharine sweetness, "we were enjoying a nice dinner before you arrived."

"Yes, I see that. I regret that I cannot join you," she began.

"You weren't invited."

Aisling and Frankie turned their fearful gazes to me, and I tried to smile in reassurance.

"I was willing to ignore your rudeness and assume that you would have offered. It seems, however, that I have some preparations to which I must attend." Without another word or glance, she swept from the café.

"Whoa," Lily whispered. "She just *felt* evil."

"Aye," Frankie assented.

Aisling still didn't speak.

"I think she might be worse than my mom," Lily continued, a small smile playing at her lips. "Yes, yes, I think she's worse. Perhaps we should introduce them. Mother could do with a friend."

Aisling cracked a hesitant grin, but I laughed out loud and pulled Lily close.

"You're the bravest girl I know." I pressed my lips to the shell of her ear.

She dipped her head toward me and accepted a kiss. Frankie and Aisling grinned widely, and the chill from Morrigan's visit dissipated.

*

We left Dublin early the next morning. There was a tearful farewell with Aisling, because Lily wasn't sure if she'd get to see her again before she left for college in less than a week.

Frankie wasn't in his usual spot outside the hotel, and it hurt Lily terribly that she didn't have a chance to wish him well. I tried my best to convince her that she'd be back to Ireland, and in Frankie's company again, before she knew it. The rainy weather matched our spirits as we followed Dave and Celia in our little rental car. Apparently, the audition had not gone as well as Celia had hoped. Lily was relieved to ride the four hours back to Cork without her mother's irritable company.

When we reached the Kingston, we were given our usual rooms. I wanted to comfort Lily, but I was at a loss. We sat on a bench overlooking the River Lee, glad for a brief respite from the rain. Her tears were another matter. They continued to glide silently down her cheeks. Because I could find no words, I simply held her hand in mine, caressing her knuckles.

The sun slipped below the horizon, and still we sat. Finally, around ten o'clock, Lily gave a sigh so huge that it didn't sound like it could come from her slender body.

"Thank you."

"I didn't do anything," I began, confused, but she lifted a hand to my cheek.

"You were here. That's enough."

"I thought I made it clear that I always would be," I said, frowning. "Did you not understand?"

"Yes, but thanks all the same." She stretched up to kiss me, pressing her soft lips to mine for a moment.

"If that's how you show your thanks, then you can thank me anytime," I teased.

She laughed and placed another kiss on my lips.

a naoi deag

"Rioghan!"

I heard her scream from across the hall. I was by her side instantly, not caring if I startled her. Gathering her in my arms, I whipped my head around, looking for the source of her fear, but she was alone.

"What is it, my love?" I whispered, in case the threat was still there but hiding out of sight.

"It was awful," she sobbed.

I tried to stand and make a quick perusal of her suite, but she clung to me, refusing to let me go.

"Please don't leave me. I don't want to hear it again."

"What did you hear, Lily?" My voice was too stern, my worry absolute. I tried to relax my features into loving concern, but I literally shuddered with fear.

"An awful scream," she whispered through trembling lips.

Pounding on the door made us both jump. She looked at me, stricken, knowing that I couldn't be found in her room if it was her guard, but also not wanting me to leave in case the reason for her terror was on the other side.

"Lily," a man called.

She relaxed and threw back her covers. I ducked into a shadow and nodded for her to open the door.

"Hi, Dave. Did you hear that scream?" She leaned against the doorframe wearily.

"I didn't hear anything but you, love. What's got you so frightened?" Dave was a big guy, and I'd seen how very protective he was of his charge. I believed he truly loved her, the way she always hoped to be loved by a caring adult.

"You didn't hear anyone scream before I did?" she asked, her mouth tightening in terror.

"You had a nightmare, didn't you?" Dave cupped her face in concern.

He visibly dropped his defensive stance, but his eyes searched her face carefully. He loved her the way a parent would—the parent she should have had.

"I guess that's what it was," Lily sighed.

My mind, however, turned over several ideas, and I didn't like any of them.

"Should I take a look around your room? Would it make you feel better?" Dave moved forward, eager to ease Lily's mind.

"That's okay," she sighed. "It seemed so real, that's all. But if you didn't hear it… It was so loud. I can't believe it wasn't outside my window."

She pushed herself away from the wall and took a step back into the room so Dave could peer in. I pressed myself against the wall, cursing Lily's trust in me. What if I was spotted? Dave seemed satisfied with his quick glance, and he pressed a quick kiss to her forehead.

"Get some rest, kid," he told her, his words gruff with emotion.

She waved him away, certain that the boogeyman had only been in her head.

"Sorry, Rioghan," she sighed. "I guess it was a nightmare."

"I'm not so sure." I stepped out of the shadows. I didn't want to frighten her any more, but I needed to be sure. "Tell me more about your family."

It wasn't a request, and Lily was perturbed by the command in my voice.

"You know about my stupid family. I'm an only child, which sucks. My *father* is somewhere in Colorado now and never sees me because he doesn't have the guts to face my mom. My *mother* is only that in the loosest sense of the word. She gave birth to me, she makes sure I eat, and she hangs me on her arm like I'm a pretty handbag." She stalked about the room while she talked, but with her final word, she flung herself onto the bed.

"But your dad, what was his name?" I pressed.

"Um, Ken. Why?" She looked at me like I'd grown a second head.

"Last name," I huffed impatiently, ignoring her questions for the moment.

"Bloom." She hurried to supply an answer. "What does it matter?"

"Hm. And your mother's maiden name is Murphy. Is that why she goes by Celia Murphy?" I continued.

"No. Murphy was the name of her first husband. She got famous while she was married to him, so she kept it. My father was her second husband. She's been married so many blessed times that I wouldn't even know what name to call her if she didn't keep the one." She sat up, her quizzical eyes on me at all times.

"So what *is* her maiden name?" I ground out.

Lily wasn't running me in circles on purpose, but I was so impatient for her answer that I felt ready to snap.

"Well, I wouldn't even know that if I didn't get a nice little Christmas card from Granny and Grampa Kavanagh every year. I've never even met them. Mother says they're not nice people, but I can't imagine they'd be any worse than her. I don't think she wants to be reminded of how poor she was."

I let her babble, because my blood had suddenly turned to ice. I had suspected, but I hadn't expected the bloodline to be quite so potent. I had planned to quiz her all night, if need be, until I heard one of the names. I collapsed onto the edge of the bed and swore loudly.

Lily stopped her tirade mid-sentence with a shocked laugh. "Um, I've never heard you say that one before."

I couldn't return her amusement.

"Wait," she said, interpreting my expression correctly. "You know what's going on here?"

I nodded.

"Well, do ya feel like sharing?" she growled.

I wanted to smile, to reassure her, but the truth was that she was going to die. That very night. The *bean-shídh* sang for her.

"Do you know what the *bean-shídh* is?" I started slowly, hoping to keep her with me through the explanation.

"It sounded like you said banshee." Lily grimaced at the implications.

"That is the more modern term, yes."

"So I heard a banshee? Great. Isn't that, like, bad luck or something? Wait, do banshees even exist? I thought they were kind of..." She froze, staring at me with her mouth open. "A fairytale."

"Yes, the *bean-shídh* exists, and yes, you could say 'tis bad luck to hear their song. She sings for certain families, and Kavanagh is one of them," I pulled her closer, wrapping my arms around her waist. "I won't let it happen, love. Whoever comes for you can go straight to Hell, and I'll gladly send them there."

"What are you talking about?" Lily was trembling again.

"This is my fault for not being able to stay away from you. They hate you, you know, the fairies, because you're human." I couldn't put together coherent sentences, but my anger and fear kept thoughts from fully forming. "You get to go to Heaven, and they don't. Well, I don't, either. Someone has decided that they'll give you a boost, get you there all the faster."

"You're not making any sense," she complained.

"I know, love. Give me a moment to collect my thoughts." It wasn't easy to ignore the smoky blue vest and shorts she wore to sleep in, but I pushed desire aside to worry about protecting her. I buried my nose in her delicious red curls and breathed deeply to calm myself.

"I went to see my father," I started. She jumped, and the top of her head smashed my nose. I rubbed it mindlessly as I continued. "I asked him to give you a chance, you see. I told him that I don't have to ask permission, but that I wanted to. I wanted him to know you and to understand why I love you so very much. He didn't understand, but I didn't believe he would do anything to hurt you."

"Your father?" Lily asked, her eyes as wide as saucers.

I nodded, trying to smile with reassurance, but my lips wouldn't work.

"It seems my father has decided that you must die." My voice was hard as I spat the words.

What a ridiculous sentiment. If Lily was fully aware of my immortality, why couldn't we work through the problems in our own way? It seemed that none of my kind should find a problem with the situation, as it did not affect them directly. But, no. I had the audacity to fall in love with a mortal—a beautiful, selfless, broken, and strong mortal. Though I should live the remainder of eternity without her once she passed on to the next life, I had chosen to cling to the years that we did have. To me, they would be as the blink of an eye.

"I still don't understand," Lily whispered.

I pulled her into my lap, and she curled into my embrace, laying her head upon my shoulder. She shook so hard I could barely hold her, so I soothed her with a quick charm.

"I won't allow it to happen. I'll be right here with you and will fight off whatever may come." I cursed myself for not being better prepared. I had nothing but my bare hands with which to fight.

At that moment, a spine-chilling screech sounded through the room. Lily clutched at me, burying her face into my neck.

"Send her out, Rioghan," a voice commanded. "There's no reason to hurt you if you release her willingly."

"You wouldn't hurt me anyway, for fear of my father's wrath," I called back, forcing a scornful laugh with false bravado. I was scared for my girl beyond words, but I could never allow that to show, not when my name and rank were my only weapons.

"We'll give you an hour to say your goodbyes. That seems fair," the guttural voice answered.

Dalbhach. I might have known, I thought. He was only one step away from being a demon. I must have said his name aloud, because Lily stiffened in my arms again.

"Dullvok?" she asked. "That sounds creepy."

"You don't know the half of it," I muttered. "He won't stop until you're dead. And me, for he'll have to come through me to get to you."

"But you're immortal. How can you possibly be killed?"

"There are ways," I told her grimly. The truth was, there was only one way, but my father was the keeper of that secret. Dalbhach had the dagger; I had no doubt.

"I should probably tell you this now. I do love you." Lily buried her face in my neck after dropping that bombshell.

I blinked, and her words filled my heart with such hope that death was no longer an option. "You've never…"

She smiled sadly. "I thought you knew. I'm so transparent. I should have told you a million times. I feel so stupid for not saying it every chance I had. Can I say it over and over for the next hour, instead of goodbye?"

"We aren't saying our farewells yet. I won't make this easy for them. It seems Father's sent only the one to take care of us, but Dalbhach does have a rather insidious weapon at his disposal. If I have a moment to disarm him, we could end it quickly and run, but then we'll always have to run. I'm so sorry that I've put this on your shoulders. You should be allowed the chance at a normal life, and I had to go and destroy that hope." The truth of my words hit me fully and I ducked my head in shame. "I'll never forgive myself for this."

"Stop. I will go anywhere with you," she said. "Normal life isn't a life, not since I found you. Tell me what I can do to help."

I couldn't even begin to think of a strategy. The confession she'd made still had me reeling inside. I wanted to run, and sing, and pull the stars down from the sky for our own personal fireworks display and curse myself into the darkest depths of oblivion for putting her in such a dangerous situation. My whole being struggled with the two desires as she stared at me with quizzical eyes.

"With Dalbhach watching, there's no time to move you somewhere else. Even if I could do it without him knowing, there's no way I could leave you there until I've taken care of him. I wouldn't be able to concentrate, knowing you were alone." I thought aloud, trying to make a solid plan that would result in survival for us both. "To escape now would start a whole lifetime of running, even longer for me. We'll have to stick together. When the time comes, you must lock yourself away in the washroom and do not open the door for anything. I know they can get in there as easily as walking through the wall, but maybe I can keep them at bay long enough to get the dagger."

"The dagger?" Lily breathed.

"One thing at a time, love. If I can get the dagger, it will be a short fight. If I can't, then…" I couldn't finish my thought.

"We can ask room service for a knife," Lily offered with a puzzled smile.

I laughed hollowly. "Not any knife will do, my heart. The *Fragarach* is ancient and one of a kind. Adam himself forged it in the fires of hatred and vengeance. The demon Azazel was delighted to assist with the design and creation of the most deadly weapon in all existence."

Lily settled into her usual listening position, and I yearned for the weeks we'd spent sharing without fear. She sat gingerly on the edge of the bed and crossed her legs underneath her, propped her elbow on her knee, and placed her cheek in her hand. It was such a normal thing that I could almost forget the danger that was coming for us. Almost.

"When Adam and Eve were essentially cut off from God, Adam's fury and hostility toward the serpent consumed him. He searched for a way to destroy him. The problem was the serpent wasn't an ordinary animal. He was a demon and couldn't be killed. Adam begged Azazel for help, believing Azazel to be an avenging angel. No angel would truly give help to a human bent on destroying any kind of life. The decision to give or take life rests in the hands of one alone. Vitriol clouded Adam's entire being, and he was so twisted with grief over his separation from God that clear thought was an impossibility.

"The dagger was created from stone taken from the Garden, and it is the only one of its kind. No other weapon of such destructive power has ever been created, and none ever will again, since the Garden has been lost forever. I believe this to be a Divine decision."

"And this dagger, you think Dalbhach will have it?" Lily asked, trying her hardest to follow what should never have been explained.

"My father has been the guardian of the *Fragarach* for over ten thousand years, save for a short time when it was lost at the bottom of a forsaken lake. I know Dalbhach will have it," I said, my tone resigned.

There was no way to fight, no way to even begin to protect her. I pulled her close and pressed my lips to her temple, appreciating the smooth silk of her skin as never before. She lifted her chin, and my nose skimmed the apple of her cheek. Her sweet sigh invited me to slide my lips over her jaw to claim her mouth.

Instead of a gentle, innocent kiss, she opened immediately, welcoming me. I resisted the rush of desire, instead reveling in her faith. She trusted me to hold her, to protect her, to love her for however long we had left. Her supplication was a sign that she was ready to give me everything, but I couldn't take.

My fingers twisted in her hair, the curls tickling my skin and reminding me that she was innocent, so innocent. I delved with my tongue, tasting her and leading her, but never giving in to the want that rippled below the surface.

My only hope to keep her alive was to get that dagger. If I failed, those would be our last moments together. I concentrated on the fragrance of her hair, the smell of her cheek, the line of her earlobe, committing them all to memory. I reveled in the feel of her arms around me, the warmth of her breath on my neck, the pressure of her fingertips at my waist.

"If I get to Heaven," Lily whispered.

"You will," I hissed.

She tipped her head and smiled at me sadly. "When I get to Heaven, I will tell them that they're missing the best and brightest angel of them all. That you laid down your life to save mine, and that if that isn't good enough for Heaven, I don't know what could be."

"When you get to Heaven, years and years from now, *you* will be the best and brightest. This is not the end for you, Lily, I swear it."

At that moment a frantic knock sounded at the door.

a fiche

"Dave?" Lily called.

I glanced at the clock. Our time was up. I hoped it *was* Dave, and that Dalbhach hadn't decided to come through the halls of the hotel and risk human witnesses to the impending battle.

"Emm, no," a small voice sounded from the other side of the door. "It's me, Lily. Can I come in?"

"Ciarán?" she called, standing quickly. "Ciarán, honey, what are you doing here?"

"I can't tell you, Lily. You'll have to let me in. Please? Hurry."

More tricks? Had Dalbhach been watching when Lily and I spent time with our little friend? Would he use this disguise as a way to gain easy entrance?

The questions surfaced and disappeared. I didn't have much time to ponder, as Lily's hand was already on the knob. I flashed to her side as she opened the door.

What I saw made me fling Lily to the other side of the room with a growl. I knew I had probably hurt her, but it was far preferable to the alternative. Ciarán pushed me roughly out of the way and hurled himself across the bed toward the far wall. In his hand glinted the silver handle of lore—the *Fragarach*.

"Demon." I spat the worst insult I could think of and launched myself after him.

"No. Rioghan, wait," he yelled, as my hand found purchase on his ankle.

He kicked out viciously, crunching the bones in my nose. In my shock, I let go, cursing him. To my astonishment, he launched himself through the plate glass window, holding the dagger high over his head. I froze in absolute stupefaction. I heard Lily moaning from the other side of the room, which spurred me back into action. I scooped Lily into my arms, shielding her from the flying shards and the scene before us that I still didn't quite understand.

Ciarán wrestled with something in mid-air, eight floors up from the ground. I watched in horror as the little boy we had grown to love slashed violently with the stone weapon. Dalbhach's head dropped from sight, followed by the rest of his body. Ciarán flew back into the room and threw the *Fragarach* to the ground as if it burned him.

"What is this?" I snarled.

I didn't wait for a response before I grabbed the small knife to study it. I knew immediately that it was genuine. The ancient stone blade held the blood of less fortunate immortals in the fissures, and the handle of pure silver was so worn the original carving was lost for all time. I held the proof in my hand, and had seen it with my own eyes with the death of Dalbhach, but my brain could not reconcile the image

"We've come to help," Ciarán said. "More will be coming."

"How do you know any of this?" I roared, casting about in my overtaxed mind for some explanation. My movements stilled as the realization occurred to me.

"Ciarán?" The name was a whisper. I released Lily and stood slowly.

"The original." He grinned his goofy nine-year-old grin as he transformed before my eyes. Lily gave a muffled shriek behind me and scrambled backward over the bed. After a moment of silence, she crawled across the duvet and joined us again.

"Ciarán?" she whispered.

The change should have been more than she could handle, but she stood straight and fearless as she examined the muscular, blond fairy in her presence.

"Little Ciarán?" she said again, touching his cheek with reverence.

My eyes narrowed at the awe on her face. Ciarán had been lauded for centuries as one of the most beautiful beings in existence. Even with the impending fight with my father's soldiers, there was room in my mind for jealousy.

"You were cuter as a chubby little boy," Lily stated, dropping her hand abruptly. I snickered, the feeling of relief overcoming the last of my fears.

"So, who's we?" Lily asked, picking up on a phrase that I'd missed. "You said, 'we've come to help.'"

"Oi," Ciarán called, sounding like the little boy he'd been impersonating for the previous few months.

Shock overwhelmed me once again as mousy Aisling and dirty Frankie entered the room. Lily rushed forward to embrace her friends, then stood back and ogled as they transformed.

Aisling was Aoife, which I found blatantly ironic. Aoife was undoubtedly one of the most beautiful of God's creations, with her billowing caramel curls and clear azure eyes. To think that she had sacrificed her fairy form for the drab, lifeless Aisling was laughable. Frankie, good-natured, loveable, stinky Frankie, became Fechín. The scraggly beard, tangled grey hair, and grizzled face were all gone and in their place were a strong jaw, jet black hair that hung to his shoulders, and a smooth, wide forehead.

Lily looked as though she didn't know whether to feel betrayed or grateful.

"I can't believe that I wished for all of you to be happy. I prayed daily that you would someday be loved, and cared for, and..." She broke off, her voice strangled. "And look at you. You didn't need my concern. You're all gorgeous. You can all strike someone dead for being mean to you."

Understanding crossed Aoife's face first. Even I was still staring at Lily like she might sprout another head.

"Lily, love. I'm sorry I deceived you. I know it doesn't help matters when I say I did it unwillingly, that I was ordered to watch you. But I have been nothing but honest when it comes to my feelings for you. You've been the best friend I've ever had, or will ever have."

Her words were tender and filled with pain. I felt a twinge of kinship with her, for it was obvious she was as forever transformed by the Lily-girl as I was.

"It was nice to be loved, not because I'm beautiful or powerful, but because of who I am. I've known from the beginning that you seek that kind of friendship, too, and it made our bond so much stronger."

"What did you mean, you were ordered to watch her?" I interrupted. Lily still needed time to process that new information, so I felt no guilt in stepping in.

"Your father has been aware of your infatuation," Fechín began.

"I love her," I growled.

Fechín held up his hands in apology. "We know. You have from the moment you met her, this much has become clear. Your father was sure it was an infatuation and would fade. But then Ciarán thought it would be funny to see what happened if you realized that you were falling in love."

"Oh, you're bloody hilarious," I said dryly, remembering the very moment I discovered my true feelings for her. He had been standing right behind me in the library. Ciarán shrugged his shoulders and sheepishly kicked at an invisible spot on the floor.

"Why is that so funny?" Lily asked.

I sighed, knowing that she had already absorbed so much. At any moment, with one new bit of information, she might run screaming and check herself into the nearest mental hospital.

"Ciarán hasn't always been Ciarán," Aoife tried to explain. "Well, I've not always been known as Aoife, either. Help, Rioghan?"

"Ciarán's more popular name is Cupid," I ground out.

My eyes were locked on Ciarán's as I debated the pros and cons of punching him in the nose.

Lily snorted in laughter. "Cupid? Like the little baby with the diaper and the bow and arrow?"

"More like the heedless, irresponsible child who thinks it's bleedin' hysterical to turn people's lives upside down," I corrected.

"I'm no child," Ciarán said boldly, drawing himself up to his full height.

Lily was still giggling uncontrollably, and I wondered if she had finally reached that breaking point I so feared.

"Are you all right, there?" I put a calming hand on her shoulder.

"I honestly don't know," she said, hiccuping and wiping at the tears in the corners of her eyes. "It's all just…so much. There's this—" she gestured at the broken glass on the floor, "—and him."

She hooked a thumb over her shoulder toward the window where Dalbhach had disappeared sans head. "And then all of you. I know you're here to help, and I shouldn't be angry. But I'm just *shocked.* I feel like I might be in shock."

"It's okay, love. We'll all get through this, and then you can make fun of Cupid all you want."

Fechín cleared his throat and looked put out. I gestured imperiously to let him know the floor was his, and he continued.

"So he sent me, and we all know how that turned out. He was sure that Lily would ignore a homeless waif—that she would never bother to show me any notice. I even covered myself in disgusting things to further repel her. Rioghan, you can't imagine. Her heart is too pure, but we couldn't make your father see this. Aoife was the final straw, I'm afraid. We only served to anger him more, and for that I will forever be sorry."

"You're spies? You're really spies?" Lily sputtered, quivering with rage.

Her helpless giggles had disappeared completely, and in their place was a scowl so fierce that it sent chills down my spine. I put a restraining arm around her, but it wasn't necessary. She was paralyzed by her wrath.

"Please forgive us, Lily," Aoife began.

"To forgive is Divine," Ciarán added, a mischievous smile crossing his lips.

A snarl ripped from Lily's throat, and she moved faster than I believed possible. In an instant, she ran headlong across the room, her shoulder aimed at Ciarán's mid-section. He threw back his head in laughter as he caught her easily.

Holding her by the shoulders, he looked deeply into her eyes. I held my breath, jealous of his close proximity and prayerful that he would be able to reason with her. After all, we had no idea how much time was at our disposal before the second attack began. My father would certainly know that his mightiest and most obedient soldier had fallen.

"Lily, my friend," he started, holding a hand up when she made an impatient noise. "We are very sorry to have deceived you. We are so grateful for the selfless love, compassion, and friendship that you have offered to us and will forever remember the times of fun and laughter that you have shared. In this short amount of time, you have become the most important person, not only in Rioghan's life, but mine as well. I don't have to ask Aoife or Fechín if they feel the same way, because by being here, willing to protect you from powers that you can't even begin to imagine, they are pledging their devotion to you. I won't take away your right to anger. I won't ask you to forgive yet. I would, however, like very much if we could set this aside for a few hours so that we might discuss a way to keep you alive?"

Lily held Ciarán's gaze throughout his speech, and her posture drooped with acceptance. I sighed with relief and moved quickly into action. As I crossed the room to close the curtains, I could see Lily embracing Aoife, Ciarán, and Fechín in turn. She must have decided to dispense with the righteous indignation and move forward.

"Do we have a plan?" Fechín asked me.

"Why would I have a plan? I didn't know this was going to happen. Ciarán seems to be the one with all the facts, since he managed to swipe the dagger. Why don't you ask him?"

Ciarán snapped his fingers, as if something had just occurred to him. "Your father will not be very happy with me. In fact, I'd go so far as to say he might kill me."

Lily's eyes widened and she gasped. "No."

"Please explain," I demanded tersely.

Ciarán looked at everything except my face, so I knew there was something he hadn't told me.

"That dagger is constantly guarded by my father's strongest and most skillful. There's no chance you managed to slip in unnoticed. Which means…"

"He gave it to me, yes," Ciarán finished.

My grip tightened around the silver handle as I stared at him through narrowed eyes. Lily put a calming hand on my arm and nodded for Ciarán to continue.

"He wanted me to kill you, Rioghan. That's why he gave me the dagger."

My heart stopped beating for a full second and the room shimmered around me. Why did my father want me dead? Was it so embarrassing for the Prince of Fairies to fall in love with a girl?

"You defied him," Fechín explained. "Lily was never the problem—not the root of the problem. He realized that he was losing you, the heir, to the human world long before you met Lily.

With you eliminated, he could rightfully choose his heir and know that his will would be carried on."

"What's the point of him having an heir?" Lily wanted to know. "I mean, he's not going to die anyway, right?"

"I imagine that it's very much the same with your mother," I explained bitterly. "I am not someone to love and nurture. I am someone who should agree with him, make him look good, and carry on his ridiculous laws. Whether he dies or not isn't the issue."

Lily's expression told me that she understood. She turned back to Ciarán for the rest of his story.

"So your father gave me the chance to redeem myself. He called me to the throne room this morning and explained the situation. He had the dagger brought from the vaults and made me vow upon the sanctity of your mother that I would use it to destroy you."

"Why would you do that?" I snapped.

"Relax, Rioghan. I didn't mean a word of it in the first place, but even if I did, I imagine your mother would give up her place in Heaven to make sure you remained safe. Either way, I didn't mind lying to him."

"You seem to be under the mistaken impression that my own father planning my demise should be a cheerful subject to me," I growled.

"Oh, well, there's that," Ciarán said, looking properly abashed.

"He's gone too far," I exploded. "His intoxication with his power is beginning to rival that of Lucifer's."

My companions gasped, even Lily, at the blasphemy of my words, but I spoke the truth. My father had once been good. He'd been one of the Father's very best, in fact, and his favor with the Lord had been the reason for his rise to power once we were Earth-bound. But power corrupts, and greed is the root of evil. In the span of a few short centuries, my father had become nothing better than the ruler of Hell himself.

With a deep, shuddering breath, I calmed myself. Ciarán sensed I was ready to hear the rest.

"He intended for me to destroy you first and let Dalbhach handle Lily. I don't know how I managed to convince him I could be trusted, especially after learning that Dalbhach might touch her."

He turned to Lily with a tender smile. "I love you, too, you see. Not in the same manner as Rioghan, but just as much. The idea of any harm coming your way…"

My heart swelled for my ancient friend.

"Anyway," Fechín interrupted, "we now have the dagger and greater numbers on our side. Ciarán called us immediately to ask for our help, and we are here. He was speaking the truth when he said there will be more, so we must discuss our battle plan."

"Fechín is a great warrior," I whispered to Lily.

I held Lily in my arms as we plotted and planned, caressing her hair at regular intervals. I intended to calm her, but the action was as reassuring to me as it was meant to be for her. She knew nothing of war, so our talk of strategy was beyond her experience. To distract, and maybe even to calm, herself, she first began to play with the comforter on the bed, then an invisible piece of lint on her nightclothes, and finally the handle of the dagger I held clenched in my fist.

"So this is the great *Fragarach*," Lily murmured with awe, taking the knife from me.

I relinquished it, smiling at the absurd picture of perfect, human Lily holding a weapon of such immense capability and antiquity. The image would not reconcile itself.

"This is it. Though you know the actual origin, you may be surprised to learn that you've heard stories of its greatness before. Though I believe you call it something else?"

She narrowed her eyes quizzically for a moment, then gasped as the realization hit. "Excalibur? I'm holding Excalibur? The really, real Excalibur?"

We all smiled at her excitement.

"But I thought it was a huge sword? Almost like a claymore?"

"Ah, that's the myth, isn't it?" I sighed. "I'd say it's rather like a fishing story, no? Every time someone tells the story, it gets bigger and bigger."

"Huh. This does kind of dampen the legend." Her slender fingers lost their grip on the handle for a moment, and Ciarán, Fechín, Aoife and I all jumped out of the way of the deadly blade.

"Take it back before she does something stupid," Ciarán pleaded.

fiche a haon

Aoife and Fechín made us aware of my father's intention to send six more of his strongest soldiers to ensure Ciarán had played his role, which would certainly leave us short-handed. Even if Lily was allowed to stand against them, and there wasn't a chance in hell of that happening, we were still grossly outnumbered. Our only chance was to circumvent the assassins and face my father head-on. When the plans were as final as we could manage, I turned to Lily.

"Ciarán and I will take you to safety and meet Fechín and Aiofe at the palace."

"I'm sorry," she said, standing slowly. "You're going to shuffle me off somewhere out of the way so you won't have to worry about me? That's not fair, Rioghan."

"Please, Lily," I begged. "There's no time to argue. The point is that you are destructible. We are not. We have the dagger, yes, but we cannot count on keeping it long enough to end the fight before you're in danger."

"I don't like this plan," she huffed, wrinkling her nose.

I pulled her close and kissed the top of her head, enjoying the feel of her in my arms for what could be the last time. "I know, love. But I must know that you are safe. We can win this."

"I have no doubt in any of you," she said with a reassuring smile. She stepped out of my embrace and approached Fechín.

"You're a dear. Keep yourself safe, please?" she asked, placing a kiss on his cheek.

"They'll not harm me," Fechín promised. A rush of color filled his cheeks at her open display of affection.

"Where's mine?" Ciarán asked, turning his face to present his cheek.

"You're going where I'm going," Lily reminded him. "You'll get yours when we get there."

"Fair enough," Ciarán said with a nod.

There was a knock at the door, and we all froze. It wasn't Father's style to enter through the front door; he would have some strategy of surprise for us.

Lily was already at the door, awaiting my signal. Aoife hovered close by, looking at me for reassurance.

"Lily?" a voice called.

I relaxed and nodded for her to open the door.

"It's my bodyguard," Lily whispered.

"Lily?" he called again. "Open up, love."

"Just a sec, Dave," she responded. We all hustled to the bathroom. When we were out of sight, she let Dave in. Aoife watched long enough to make sure Dave was alone before closing the door with a quiet click.

We listened closely but could only make out quiet murmurs. I was sure Lily would try to reassure him as quickly as possible and send him on his way. Aoife examined her nails, and Ciarán checked his appearance in the mirror and straightened his eyebrows while we waited. Fechín, however, kept a warrior's stance, ready for action at any second. I caught his eye and smiled gratefully.

The murmurs from the other room grew closer, but we couldn't make out what was being said through the heavy wooden door. There was no mistaking the fear in Lily's voice when she cried, "Dave, no!"

I jumped at the door, prepared to come to her defense, when it crashed open. Ciarán, Aoife, and I all froze, while Fechín jumped forward in attack mode. He, too, stopped when he saw Lily's terrified expression.

"Lily Rose Murphy, what in bleedin' hell is going on here?" Dave roared.

Lily peeked around him, her face blazing in shame and anger.

"Hi, Dave," I said calmly, throwing him a casual wave.

"Windows broken, room trashed. Are you having a party?" Dave demanded. His eyes drifted over us, widening when he saw Aoife.

"Oh, it's definitely not a party atmosphere," Ciarán said dryly. "I'm Ciarán."

"Ciarán? How many Ciaráns do you know, Lily?" Dave was lost.

Lily looked to me for guidance. I studied our friends for a moment, all of whom shifted nervously. They were as concerned with my decision as Lily was. I sighed and nodded.

"Just one," she said.

Dave had not missed the quick interaction between us, and he growled. "Someone's lying."

"No, Dave. It's a long story, and I don't think we have time to explain everything."

"Oh, just show him." Lily waved her hand, telling us to get on with it.

Ciarán pumped his fist in excitement. Transforming was one of his favorite powers, besides that whole convincing humans they were in love thing. There wasn't a sound as he slipped into the nine-year-old form, grinned playfully and waved at Dave, and then assumed his natural state again.

Lily's protector was stunned silent. Panic filled his eyes and he stumbled away from the door, swearing and rubbing his face in disbelief. When he spoke, his words were garbled and feverish, but I trusted he'd snap out of it quickly.

"You're in Ireland, mate," I reminded him. "Land of the fairies, banshees, and leprechauns. I'm afraid I've caused a stir among the magic folk of the land by falling in love with Lily. My dear ol' da, the King of the Fairies, has effectively signed my death warrant, but he wants Lily to go first so that I'm well and truly punished."

"Like hell!" Dave muttered. "I don't drink. I don't do drugs. I know I'm not dreaming."

"It's much easier if you allow yourself to suspend reality." Lily shrugged. "We've got a plan, too. We'll be okay, Dave."

"You're not going anywhere without me," Dave threatened.

"I'm afraid you can't stop us," I warned. Dave went to grab his gun, and I shook my head. "You're up against powers you'll never comprehend. That's a toy compared to what's coming for us."

Dave looked down at the weapon in his hand and shook his head as if to clear it.

"It could at least slow someone down, right?" he asked, a look of hope in his eyes.

"It could do that." I nodded, grateful for his loyalty.

"Then I'm going with you. I'm not leaving my little girl."

Lily's eyes filled with fresh tears at his assertion, and she ran forward to give him a fierce hug.

"Lily, love," Aoife started, but Lily pulled away in comprehension.

"I know. Must go."

"New plan," Fechín said, eyeing Dave with respect. "Now we have a pistol and the dagger. I don't think we can give up that advantage. If Dave can slow them, I can take care of them."

"The way the Godfather takes care of things," Ciarán muttered.

We all rolled our eyes and snickered, including Dave. He seemed to go for the plan, but he didn't yet know that Ciarán and I would be removing Lily from the action. Before we could inform him, there was a rushing of wind through the broken window. I watched it ruffle Lily's hair into a halo on her head and knew we'd run out of time.

Fechín led the way out of the bathroom, followed closely by Aoife and Dave. All three had looks of feral determination, and I was grateful for their resolve to protect my love. Ciarán and I took Lily by the arms and led her after the others. There would be one last attempt to plead our case. If that should fail, Ciarán and I were prepared to whisk Lily away immediately.

"Human?" a voice laughed.

Scathach's gravelly tone filled the room. He had been Dalbhach's closest compatriot and would certainly seek revenge. Our intention to talk first seemed silly; the night could end in a bloodbath. Ainbheartach and Fachtna stood to each side of him. I was surprised they were the extent of the force sent for me. Perhaps my father had underestimated us.

"You stand against us with a *human?*" Scathach asked again, an ugly sneer crossing his otherwise handsome features.

Ainbheartach and Fachtna laughed with him, the sound rough and offensive. Their eyes moved constantly, trying to deduce which of us held the *Fragarach*. Their eyes settled on Fechín, and they nodded almost imperceptibly.

The gun sounded before any of us had time to register the enemy's attack. Dave's aim was true, and Scathach fell to the ground. The wound on his bare chest began to close as his fellow soldiers pinned Fechín to the wall. Ciarán stepped forward, brandishing the dagger, and removed Scathach's head in one swift movement.

Dave's face registered fear for the first time at the same moment Ainbheartach and Fachtna realized they had misread the situation. They released Fechín and leapt for Ciarán, who danced lightly across the bed. The grin on his face indicated that he was enjoying himself, but when his eyes skittered over to Lily, I knew his fear for her would keep him on track.

Dave aimed again, and Fachtna fell.

Ciarán changed his direction and relieved Fachtna of his head without a sound. With a roar of fury, Ainbheartach launched himself at Ciarán. We all froze as his open-fisted attack found purchase. The *Fragarach* slipped from Ciarán's grasp and, in a flash of silver and stone, bounced across the floor.

Every person in the room dove for the dagger, including Lily and Dave. For several gut-wrenching seconds, we were a writhing mass on the floor. Our only hope was to get to the knife before Ainbheartach. One by one, each of us backed away in confusion. The despair in Ainbheartach's face told me he had not retrieved the dagger. Ciarán and Fechín cursed, Dave searched the ground fruitlessly, and Aoife watched Ainbheartach to assure that he wasn't attempting to fool us.

The *Fragarach* was no longer where it had landed. Someone had it, but no one admitted to holding it. I snapped Lily up into my arms and turn on the spot. Dave's gun roared, and a searing pain shot through my arm as we disappeared from the hotel suite.

When we reappeared in *Tír na nÓg*, I discovered cause my pain. Ainbheartach clutched my shoulder with all his might. He had followed us. The dagger was in the hotel room, and the enemy with us. I tossed Lily for the second time that night and turned to Ainbheartach with a snarl.

A small hole above his ribs was closing, and I felt a rush of pride that Dave had managed to get another shot in. My adversary was still in pain, and I had to use that advantage before the injury healed. Without thinking, I thrust my thumb into the wound. Ainbheartach's shrieks echoed off the imperturbable stone, and I placed a well-aimed punch to his open mouth. Blood gushed over my knuckles, a mixture of his and my own.

He responded with his own strike, and I saw stars as my head rang from his immense strength. He was a warrior, and I was a pampered prince. If I didn't keep one step ahead of him, I had no hope of outmaneuvering him.

In desperation, I continued to rain punches upon him. The bullet wound had already closed, so I had no choice but to create new injuries. I slowly lost ground against his superior training.

Lily called my name over and over. I wanted to give her some reassurance that I was okay, but I couldn't take my eyes off Ainbheartach. He would destroy her the moment he found reprieve. Just beyond my field of vision, she moved closer with determined steps.

I did the stupidest thing I had ever done. I took my eyes off my opponent. In that split second, Lily was upon us, right before a massive fist crashed into the side of my head. The stars gave way to darkness.

I awoke in a panic. Someone was crying, and cool fingers ran through my hair. I started to open my eyes, but then I heard laughter. There should be no laughter. I had lost sight of the attacker. I had lost.

"Unbelievable. A whole army of immortal beings, and the human wins the battle," the voice said.

My eyes popped open to see Lily hovering over me.

"Oh, thank God. That was such a hard hit. I knew you'd be okay, but I was still scared." She smiled at me tenderly through her tears.

I took stock of my limbs and judged I was well on my way to healed.

Ciarán, Fechín, and Aoife watched us with bright smiles. I looked around and found Ainbheartach lying on his side about ten feet away. His head was at an unnatural angle, suggesting it wasn't attached anymore.

"That was the way to kill him, wasn't it?" Lily lifted the *Fragarach* sheepishly and gestured at the fallen foe.

"The most effective, yes," Ciarán said.

"What took you guys so long?" I finally spoke.

"We had to convince Dave that he would better serve by getting rid of the bodies in the hotel room. Celia is going to have a fit over that window," Aoife snickered.

"Well, let's finish this," I said, my words ringing with finality.

fiche a do

To anyone but my father, we would have been an impressive and fearful sight. I led the way, while Aoife flanked Lily behind me. Cairan and Fechín stood tall and proud in the rear, guarding our group fiercely. I threw open the door to the throne room and entered with sure steps. I would find my father there; it was where he always stayed during battle.

"Rioghan, my son, it's good to see you. And Lily, how delightful that you've come to visit me again."

"Leave it out, Father." I bit the words out harshly as I came to a halt in front of the platform where he sat.

Lily and Aoife remained behind, but Ciarán and Fechín moved to stand with me.

"I see you've failed me, Ciarán," Ailbhe said, his voice as rich as velvet. He sounded as if he complimented my friend.

"Not failed, no," Ciarán stated cheerfully. "Defied, yes. And I would do it again, gladly."

"You realize that in doing so, you have sealed your fate?" my father asked, raising an eyebrow. He showed no more emotion than he would at the dinner table.

"I had assumed as much," Ciarán said brightly.

Fechín coughed to hide his laughter. That disrespectful act sent my father into a rage.

"How dare you? All of you! You, *human*," he roared, "what makes you think you're *worthy* of the Prince of Fairies? And Rioghan, how could you surrender your birthright for a daughter of Eve, the original deceiver? The three of you, my favorite guardians, you…"

"I have no doubt that I'm not worthy of his love," Lily assured him.

Ailbhe was so shocked she dared speak, he broke off mid-sentence and stared.

"You are, love," I whispered, squeezing her hand.

"No, but isn't this the point of unconditional love? None of us are worthy. Wasn't it a merciful God who loved Adam and Eve after the fall?"

"Merciful," Ailbhe spat, finding his voice again. "That merciful God has banished us here for all eternity. My own love sits on the other side of the gates, inches from my grasp. Ten thousand years I have walked this miserable rock, yearning to be with her. Pleading, praying, begging and bargaining with a God who refuses my fondest wish."

"And you love her still?" Lily asked.

"How *dare* you?" my father seethed.

"Because one day, Rioghan and I will suffer the same fate. You can't possibly know how many times I've wished that he would find someone of his own kind he could love. Someone who could stand next to him always, the way I'll never be able to. But one day he'll be lost here forever while I move on. This thought is not comforting to me, except in one fact. We love anyway."

What she said made perfect sense, but I was still consumed with her vision of my future. Another ten thousand years without her? The thought was absolutely unbearable. For a moment, I could sympathize with my father's all-encompassing wrath.

"How can you expect to understand?" my father roared.

Lily took a step back, but did not show fear on her face. He lunged at her, wrapping his long, bony fingers around her throat.

"You speak to me as if you believe you have the wisdom of the millennia. You are but a child, and even if you were allowed a long and fruitful life, you would still be as a child."

I reached forward in a panic, knowing that Lily was far too fragile to be handled that way. He could easily kill her with a flick of his wrist. Her face turned blue as I worked at my father's fingers.

"Release her," I commanded, but he ignored me.

An animalistic snarl echoed through the room, ripped from my throat without my knowledge. I was dimly aware of Aoife, Ciarán, and Fechín pulling at Lily, trying to free her from Ailbhe's iron grip. It was no use, and Lily's eyes began to protrude from their sockets.

"You're killing her!" I screamed, attacking my father with renewed fervor.

Desperate to end her suffering, I kicked and screamed like a man possessed. Seething red obscured my vision, roaring hatred filled my ears. I flung my fists, bloodying my father's nose with one punch and breaking it completely with the next. He clutched her neck, waving me away like an annoying bug until Lily collapsed.

"Demon!" I hurled at my father.

Ailbhe turned cold, triumphant eyes upon me, and fury like none I had ever known surged through me. If he killed her, I would avenge her myself. He still held her throat, looking pleased with himself when, suddenly, he went rigid. His eyes rolled back into his head, and he released his grip on Lily. I caught her as they fell but let my father hit the stone floor with a crashing thud.

"Lily," I whispered.

Her face was chalky, her limbs deathly still. The cold hand of fear grabbed my heart and squeezed mercilessly. I laid her on the stone floor and felt for a pulse. It was there, but faint. Her heart would not beat much longer.

Not now. Not her, I prayed silently.

I could save her, but to do so would damn my existence among my kind for all of eternity. My father would kill us both once he recovered. To heal her, bring her back from the brink of death, would effectively sever my ties with the Otherworld, the only world I had ever known. The decision was simple. I willed the tears away to clear vision so I could perform the task correctly.

Leaning over her, I breathed warm air through her lips and then placed my trembling hand over her heart. To a human, it would have looked like a lame attempt at CPR. Warmth emanated from the very core of my body, the rush and roar of power unfamiliar to me, and I knew it was working. As I labored, giving her my very life's essence to replace what my father had taken, I hummed the notes to the first song I had heard her sing. I hoped against hope she could hear me, that she would know I was there with her. My thoughts raced through memories—the first time I saw her at Sullivan's Pub, the sunlight bouncing off her perfect curls as she approached Cratloe Castle, the ringing of her laughter as she collapsed on the sidewalk, the glorious tone of her voice as she sang the very song I was singing for her as I worked.

A whisper of sound sent pulsing joy throughout my body. She joined me, her voice low and raspy from the damage to her throat, but that evidence she was still with us, that she would live, was the most awe-inspiring music I'd ever heard.

"Oh, Lily. You had me so worried. My love, my heart, my life!"

"Chill out, Romeo," she said with a goofy grin. "I'm fine."

The journey back from the edge of death often inspired giddy thoughts and feelings. I was glad to see she responded normally to the treatment, even if it was in direct contrast to the situation.

"Of course you are," I murmured, gathering her to my chest and breathing in the rosemary and mint of her curls. "Of course you are."

"I don't think your dad likes me much." Her giggles faded as the effects of the healing wore off, leaving a look of concern in their place.

"Damn it. Father." I turned to see my father, who had not yet risen.

"I'm sorry Rioghan," Ciarán said, staring at the ground. "I didn't feel I had a choice. He was going to kill her...and I—I couldn't let that happen. Not to Lily."

"He's dead?" I was surprised at how cold and detached I sounded.

"She's mine, too, Rioghan," Ciarán pleaded.

He held out the *Fragarach* and let it tumble from his fingers. My father's blood mingled on the ancient blade with that of Dalbhach and other less fortunate angels and demons of history.

"Thank you, Ciarán." I embraced him. "Thank you for saving her. Thank you for having the courage that I might never have found."

"But your father," he said weakly, still expecting an explosion.

"Will be greatly missed, I know. I also know that he has been miserable here, and it turned him. If he could have seen himself clearly, he would not have liked what he saw. And you saved my Lily."

"Our Lily," Aoife chimed in, lifting my girl into a standing position. Lily threw her arms around her friend and hugged her tightly.

"Thank you, all of you, for loving me so much. I never thought anyone could," she said fiercely.

Her tears, liquid jewels, slid silently down her cheeks as she embraced us each in turn. I held myself for last, and when she was finally in my arms, I lifted her and spun her in a circle.

"Nothing more to fear, Lily-girl." I traced my lips down the contour of her jaw to claim her mouth.

She clung to me, unashamed, and kissed me with a fervor that took my breath away. Even on her toes, she was too short to meet me, so I curled around her, pulling her even closer, as I relinquished my fear and sadness to the beauty of her love. When she still couldn't reach, I lifted her into my arms and wrapped her legs around my waist, holding her tightly as I dared. My heart was singing when we were interrupted by a polite "ahem." I tore my lips from hers and looked for the culprit who dared intrude on our happiness.

Aoife was grinning like a big sister who'd walked in on a compromising position. "So, what's the plan now, King Rioghan?"

Her words took a moment to sink in, and a low swear exited my lips. My friends all laughed at my reticence to fill such a role.

"Is it true?" Lily asked, her eyes wide.

"He never had time or motive enough to name a new heir," Fechín assured us. "Rioghan is the rightful king."

I cursed again. "This was not my intention. I'm not fit to be a king."

"I can think of several who may agree with you," Ciarán said. "Most notably Morrigan. I think you'll find that a new ruler will be refreshing for our kind. We've seen how our segregation from humans and the powers we possess can so easily lead to evil. Rioghan, you're the exact person to lead us into a new era of compassion, cooperation, and brotherhood with humans. The fact that you have a human love will make the way forward even smoother."

"If it were an election, I'd hire you to be my speechwriter," I grumbled.

"We have a lot to do," Fechín warned. "Not the least of which will be explaining the death of the Once and Future King. It's going to be touchy, and you'll be under a lot of scrutiny."

"Can't we tell everyone he choked on a chicken bone?" I pleaded. I was well aware that I was avoiding responsibility, just as my father had expected, but I needed a moment of levity before the crushing weight of reality lit upon my shoulders.

"We'll be right beside you," Aoife promised. "You won't face any of this alone."

I looked at Lily and knew it to be true. The love and pride in her eyes made me feel as though I could take on the entire world and win. How had I gone from Rioghan, the outcast prince, the lonely and unlovable cad, to Rioghan, King of the Fairies, surrounded by such amazing love and friendship?

"Right," I said, cupping Lily's face to kiss her once more. "To use one of your oh-so-quaint American expressions: let's do this thing."

"Spoken like a true king," she said proudly.

I took her hand, and we flung open the doors of the throne room, ready to face the world together.

Pronunciation Guide and Glossary

Rioghan [Ree'-an] *Little king*

Ailbhe [Al'-vyeh] *World king*

Ciarán [Kee'-ah-rahn] *Black*

Aisling [Ash-leen'] *Vision*

Aoife [Ee'-feh] *Radiant*

Fechín [Feh-keen'] *Warrior*

Aírdin [Ar'-deen] *Little height*

Beagán [Byag'-awn] *Little*

Dalbhach [Dul'-vok] *Guileful*

Scáthach [Skaw'-hok] *Frightening*

Ainbheartach [An'-vyer-tok] *Doer of evil deeds*

Fachtna [Fakt'-na] *Malicious*

*

a caoineadh [a keen'-eth] *lament*

a haon [ah hay'-un] *one*

a dó [ah doe] *two*

a trí [ah tree] *three*

a ceathair [ah ka'-hair] *four*

a cúig [ah koo'-ig] *five*

a sé [ah shay] *six*

a seacht [ah shockt] *seven*

a ocht [ah hookt] *eight*

a naoi [ah nee] *nine*

a deich [ah jeh] *ten*

a haon déag [ah hey'-un day'-ug] *eleven*

a dó dhéag [ah doe day'-ug] *twelve*

a trí déag [ah tree day'-ug] *thirteen*

a ceathair déag [ah ka'-hair day'-ug] *fourteen*

a cúig déag [ah koo'-ig day'-ug] *fifteen*

a sé déag [ah shay day'-ug] *sixteen*

a seacht déag [ah shokt day'-ug] *seventeen*

a ocht déag [ah hookt day'-ug] *eighteen*

a naoi déag [ah nee day'-ug] *nineteen*

a fiche [ah fih'-ah] *twenty*

a fiche a haon [ah fih'-ah ah hay'-un] *twenty-one*

a fiche a dó [ah fih'-ah ah doe] *twenty-two*

ABOUT THE AUTHOR

Jennifer M. Barry knows she's in trouble when people use her whole name, so just Jen is fine. In addition to writing and editing, she loves to drink coffee, consume entirely too much Cherry Garcia, laugh at herself on her blog, and watch live music. Jen lives in Nashville with her husband, Liam. They are serial renters who can't commit to anything except each other and a yearly trip to Ireland.

Visit her Web site at www.jennifermbarry.com